THAT OLD ZACK MAGIC

Especially for Girls Presents

THAT OLD
ZACK MAGIC

by Beth Cruise

Collier Books
Macmillan Publishing Company
New York
Maxwell Macmillan Canada
Toronto
Maxwell Macmillan International
New York Oxford Singapore Sydney

Photograph and logo copyright © 1993 by National
Broadcast Company, Inc. All rights reserved.
"Saved by the Bell"™ is a registered trademark of the
National Broadcast Company, Inc. Used under license.
First Collier Books edition 1993
Text copyright © 1993 by Collier Books, Macmillan
Publishing Company.
Cover design by Chani Yammer.

Collier Books   Maxwell Macmillan Canada, Inc.
Macmillan Publishing Company   1200 Eglinton Avenue East
866 Third Avenue   Suite 200
New York, NY 10022   Don Mills, Ontario M3C 3N1

Macmillan Publishing Company is part of the Maxwell
Communications Group of Companies.
Printed in the United States of America

Library of Congress Cataloging-in-Publication Data
Cruise, Beth.
That old Zack magic/by Beth Cruise.—1st Collier Books ed.
p.   cm.
Summary: The "Saved by the Bell" gang spends a scary
night at Bayside High investigating the legend of
Eerie Eddie.
ISBN 0-02-042761-1
[1. High schools—Fiction. 2. Schools—Fiction.]
I. Title.
PZ7.C88827Th 1993
[Fic]—dc20 92-37748

To Zack and all his magic

Chapter 1

▲ ▼ ▲ ▼ ▲

Thunder crashed and lightning crackled as Zack Morris headed for his seat in his fifth-period history class. He stopped by the window to look at the rain lashing hard against the panes. Rain in southern California was practically against the law, Zack reflected. This weather should be arrested.

He sighed gloomily as another thunderclap rumbled. This heavy storm activity was going to interfere with his favorite pastime—sleeping through class. American history with Mr. Willard Loomis was definitely Snooze City.

Of course, he *was* barely scraping by with a C in Mr. Loomis's class, and the teacher had already warned him that if he didn't ace his next term paper he'd slide right into D territory. And D grades meant an atmosphere in the Morris household that would make this storm today look like a day at the beach.

A moment later, Zack's friend A. C. Slater joined him at the window. Slater rested his muscular arms on the sill and looked down at the parking lot. As captain of the football and wrestling teams, Slater had a body that proved his commitment to daily workouts. It was enough to make more regular-size guys lose hope—not to mention girlfriends. If Slater wasn't such a good friend, Zack would definitely hate him.

Slater shook his curly head at the rain. "Sure looks bad, man."

"Yeah," Zack agreed. "Definitely not a beach day."

"Mmm," Slater said. "Too bad you left the top down on your Mustang."

"What?" Zack emitted a strangled cry and looked down, frantically searching for his '65 vintage convertible. He narrowed his hazel eyes as he peered through the rain and tried to remember where he'd parked this morning.

Slater chortled and elbowed him in the ribs. "Gotcha," he crowed.

"Very funny, Slater," Zack muttered. As the self-proclaimed king of scams at Bayside High, Zack wasn't crazy about anybody turning the tables and pulling a joke on *him*.

"Thanks, preppy," Slater said, still laughing. "*I* thought so."

A mournful voice came from behind them. "I know what you guys are laughing at," their friend

Lisa Turtle said. "And I don't think it's very nice at all. Just because someone is having a bad hair day doesn't mean you have to completely humiliate them."

Zack rolled his eyes at Slater as Lisa squinted nervously into the mirror of her mother-of-pearl compact. Lisa looked as pretty as she always did, but the African-American teen was constantly striving for the perfect fashion statement.

"We weren't laughing at your hair, Lisa," Zack told her patiently.

"Right," Slater said. "It's your *outfit* that's hysterical."

Lisa snapped her compact shut with a frown and looked down at her denim jumper and soft pink blouse. "You're right. This is definitely a fashion mistake. I have a date with Cal Everhart after school, too. It's a disaster!"

"Chill, Lisa," Slater reassured her. "I was only kidding. You look prime. Don't sweat it."

"Am I sweating, too?" Lisa wailed. "I knew I shouldn't have worn silk!"

Just then, Zack saw his girlfriend, Kelly Kapowski, swing through the door, her long, silky dark hair cascading down her back. She was walking with Jessie Spano, who not only was the president of the senior class but also possessed the longest legs at Bayside High. Kelly's deep blue eyes lit up when she saw Zack, even though they'd just had lunch together a few minutes ago.

The two girls joined the group at the window. "Hi, Lisa, hi, Zack," Jessie said.

"Uh, excuse me," Slater said. "Did I just turn into the invisible man?"

"Oh, Slater," Jessie said, unconcerned. "I didn't see you."

"I keep telling you to keep that appointment with the optometrist," Slater said with a smirk.

Jessie scowled and tossed her long, curly ponytail behind her shoulder nonchalantly. It slapped Slater in the face.

"Thanks for the hair sandwich," he muttered. "But I already had lunch."

"What do you mean, Slater?" Jessie asked. "For you, lunch lasts the entire afternoon. If you don't watch out, Mr. Monza is going to have to reinforce the gym floor for your next track meet."

Zack laughed. Jessie could flatten Slater better than anybody. She'd had enough practice at it. Even though the twosome had broken up some time ago, they still squabbled as much as when they were going steady.

As usual, it was Kelly who changed the subject. Her sweet nature couldn't stand any discord for long. "Can you believe this storm?" she asked with a shiver. "It's kind of spooky."

"Spooky?" Slater scoffed. "It's just atmospheric disturbances and heavy condensation."

"Well, those atmospheric disturbances

would make a good sound track to a horror movie," Kelly declared.

"Don't be scared, Kelly," Zack said, sliding an arm around her. "I can protect you."

"You, Zack?" Slater joked. "What are you going to do, hire a professional bodyguard? The last I heard, maniacs weren't scared off by pencil-legged preppies." His warm brown eyes crinkled at the corners as he laughed at his own joke.

Zack wasn't amused. Sometimes Slater pushed that macho act too much. Zack ran his hand through his blond hair, trying to think of a comeback, but just then, Mr. Loomis walked in, and everyone headed for their seats.

Zack slid into his usual seat next to Kelly, still nursing his grudge against Slater. Just because the guy had a few muscles didn't mean he had to throw his weight around. Of course, if Slater really *did* throw his weight around, Zack would be crushed to a pulp.

"Quiet, everyone," Mr. Loomis ordered, even though the room was practically silent. "I'd like to remind everyone that term papers are due in two weeks. Remember, I want you to take a current issue affecting our country and relate it to something we studied this term. Now let's begin."

Mr. Loomis was not one to waste time. He was known for his strict discipline. That was why it was such a major achievement to catch forty winks in his class. It took nerves of steel and the brim of a baseball cap.

Zack opened his notebook and took out his pen as Mr. Loomis began to drone about immigration quotas in the early twentieth century. After a huge lunch of macaroni-and-cheese casserole, it wasn't long before Zack's eyelids began to droop.

Boom! Zack had been sliding into sleep when a crash of thunder made him bolt upright. Then, a second later, all the lights went out.

A girl in the back gave a little scream, and the whole class gasped. It was such a dark afternoon that everyone in the class turned into spooky shadows. Zack could barely see Mr. Loomis up at the blackboard.

"Now quiet down, everyone," Mr. Loomis said. "I'm sure the lights will come on in a second. Let me continue with the great immigration wave prior to the First World War."

But instead of quieting down, the class continued to buzz and whisper. For once, the darkness had given them a cover to misbehave in Mr. Loomis's class, and they intended to take complete advantage of it.

Mr. Loomis rapped on the desk. "Class! Quiet!" But it was too dark for him to pick out any offenders, and nobody stopped talking.

Suddenly, the door of the classroom opened, and Mr. Belding, the principal of Bayside High, walked in. Hanging onto the tail of his jacket was

Samuel ("Screech") Powers. Screech was a curly haired bundle of nerves who just missed being a nerd by inches.

Mr. Belding swatted behind him. "Screech, you're safe now. Let go of my suit jacket before it turns into a forty-four long."

"Thanks, Mr. Belding," Screech said in a wobbly voice. "I thought I was lost for good. Trapped in high school. What a terrible fate for a teenager!"

Zack and his friends laughed. Screech was a good pal and a science whiz, but his leaps of logic could defeat an Olympic hurdler. His illogical brand of logic even extended to his wardrobe, which was legendary around Bayside High. Screech was one of the few people who thought that polka dots and stripes were a good match. Everyone should have been grateful that the lights were out and they couldn't see today's outfit.

"Sit down, Screech," Mr. Belding ordered. "I just popped in to reassure everyone that this power outage is temporary. Mr. Monza is working hard to get the lights back on."

"Good," Kelly said. "This storm was *already* spooky. Now it's scary."

"Don't worry, Kelly," Mr. Belding said. "Just stay put. I don't want anyone tripping down the stairs. Not to mention running into any ghosts," he added with a chuckle.

"Ghosts?" Screech squeaked.

"There aren't any ghosts," Slater said. "You're trying to scare us, Mr. Belding."

"I wouldn't want to do that, A. C.," Mr. Belding said. "So I think it's better if I don't tell you about Eerie Eddie."

"Eerie Eddie?" Zack asked. "Who's that?"

"Oh, just a student at Bayside High back in the fifties," Mr. Belding said. "It's a silly story, really. I mean, nobody believes in Eerie Eddie, right?"

"Come on, Mr. Belding," Jessie said. "Tell us the story. Who was Eddie?"

"Eddie Maracas," Mr. Belding said. "He bit the big one right here at Bayside High."

"He bit the big one?" Screech yelped. "Wow. I hope he had a big Alka-Seltzer. Those submarine sandwiches in the cafeteria are *huge.*"

"'Bit the big one' means that Eddie *died,* Screech," Slater informed him.

"How did he die, Mr. Belding?" Jessie asked.

"We want to know," Kelly urged. "I think," she added in an undertone.

Mr. Belding leaned forward and lowered his voice. "Eddie Maracas died mysteriously right here at Bayside," he said. "And some say he still haunts the east staircase. A kid in my graduating class swears he saw Eddie's ghost on the third-floor landing on a stormy day very much like this one."

A shudder ran through the class. "What was Eddie like?" Jessie asked.

"I guess today we'd call him a troubled kid from a dysfunctional family," Mr. Belding said. "Back then, we called him a hood. He was suspended from Bayside at least twelve times."

"Wow," Zack said. "That even beats *my* record."

"He was nineteen years old and still hadn't graduated," Mr. Belding said.

A flash of lightning suddenly illuminated the room, and Zack saw that every single student was hanging on Mr. Belding's words. Now, *that* was an event.

"This was his last chance," Mr. Belding continued. "He got all the teachers to pass him. Except one. The strictest teacher at Bayside High."

"I didn't know you were teaching back then, Mr. Loomis," Slater called. Mr. Loomis was young and handsome, and there was no way he could have been teaching forty years ago.

Everyone laughed a little too loudly. It felt good to break the tension.

"He was the chemistry teacher Mr. Snipe," Mr. Belding said. "Eddie came to see him after school and threatened him. Eddie was a big guy, but Mr. Snipe wasn't intimidated. He told Eddie to get along to detention. And he told him to help him carry some cartons of textbooks to the supply room on the way. They started down the third-floor hall and reached the top of the east staircase. Eddie was still arguing with Mr. Snipe."

Mr. Belding pitched his voice even lower. "Nobody knows what happened next. It was a rainy day, and the floors were probably pretty slick from everybody's wet shoes and umbrellas. Eddie slipped on the top step and went over the railing. Mr. Snipe rushed to help him, but he was still carrying a carton of chemistry books. He dropped the carton, and it fell on Eddie's head just after he hit the floor. Nobody ever knew what killed him—the fall or the books."

"Wow," Lisa breathed.

"There was only one thing everybody knew for sure," Mr. Belding concluded in an ominous tone. "Eddie was the type to hold a grudge."

The class sat frozen in their seats as thunder crashed again. Zack felt Kelly's hand steal over and nestle into his. He squeezed her fingers for reassurance.

"Ever since that day," Mr. Belding said, "on stormy days, strange things sometimes happen at Bayside. The windows will fly open in the chemistry lab. Someone will find a carton of books overturned on the second-floor landing. Mr. Monza has to be careful and make sure no strange puddles form on the top step on the east stairs. And sometimes"—Mr. Belding paused dramatically—"sometimes, if you listen really hard, you can hear Eddie's harmonica playing an Elvis tune. And then you just might hear Eddie's footsteps in those motorcycle boots he used to wear, coming closer and closer...."

Suddenly, they heard them...footsteps—
heavy footsteps—heading slowly down the hall.
Kelly squeezed Zack's hand so tightly he thought his
bones would break. The whole class sat paralyzed,
listening to the heavy footsteps come closer and
closer still.

Suddenly, the door flew open. DeeDee
Horwitzer screamed, and Kelly gasped as they all
saw a tall, menacing figure loom in the doorway.

"It's Eddie!" Screech shrieked.

Chapter 2

▲ ▼ ▲ ▼ ▲

A creepy hand rose in the air. The class gasped as it swung out and hit the light switch. The room was flooded with light, and Eerie Eddie turned into cranky Mr. Monza, the head of the maintenance staff.

"My name is Fernando, not Eddie," he growled. "And that's Mr. Monza to all of you," he said to the class.

"I see we got the power back," Mr. Belding said.

"I fixed the fuse box," Mr. Monza said. "It's never been the same since somebody overheated all the microwaves in home ec and blew all the fuses." He looked pointedly at Screech.

Screech sank down in his chair. Who knew that marshmallow burritos would end up exploding like that?

"I hope the blackout didn't disrupt classes too much," Mr. Monza said gruffly to Mr. Belding.

"Well, I managed to keep *one* class in order," Mr. Belding said jovially. "I heard them as I was coming down the hall, so I decided to pop in and divert them with a tall tale."

"Wait a second," Jessie said. "What do you mean, Mr. Belding?"

"Are you saying there's no Eerie Eddie after all?" Slater asked, looking relieved.

"Exactly." Mr. Belding looked extremely pleased with himself.

"You mean there's no ghost?" Screech asked. "Shucks. I was going to try to catch him."

"There's no ghost, Screech," Mr. Belding assured him. "There's only a faulty fuse box."

"Well, *that's* a relief," Kelly said. "I was never going to use those east stairs again."

Everyone in the class relaxed. Even Zack had to admit that he hadn't been totally comfortable with the thought that there might be a ghost with an armload of chemistry books at the ready to dump on some poor unsuspecting student's head.

He looked over at Slater. Slater was grinning as though he hadn't been scared for even one second, but Zack knew differently. He'd sounded awfully relieved when Mr. Belding had confessed that he'd made Eerie Eddie up. He'd been just as scared as everyone else.

The bell rang, and everyone bent to retrieve their books. Zack watched Slater thoughtfully as he strode from the classroom with that cocky, athletic walk. It was about time someone pricked that macho balloon. And Zack was just the guy to do it.

▲   ▼   ▲

After school, Lisa burst into the Max, the gang's favorite hangout. She saw Jessie and Slater sharing a pizza in the gang's usual booth, and she headed for them.

"What are you doing here, Lisa?" Jessie asked. "I thought you had a date with Cal."

"I did," Lisa said, sinking into the booth with a sigh. "But I don't know how to tune an engine. And even if I *did* know how to tune an engine, I couldn't do it in this outfit. And even if I *did* know how to do it and I was wearing the *right* outfit, I *still* wouldn't want to do it on a date! Not to mention somebody else's. Date, I mean. Not car."

"Lisa, what are you talking about?" Slater asked patiently.

"I'm talking about Cal's neighbor Cissy Garlock," Lisa said with a sigh. "She's a junior at Bayside. She's lived next door to Cal since they were babies, and they're like brother and sister. She's a really nice kid. And I hate her guts!"

"That's not like you, Lisa," Jessie said, laughing.

"Well, I don't *really* hate her guts," Lisa

admitted. "I know she doesn't mean to be annoying, but she keeps horning in on my dates with Cal. She's a real tomboy, and she's always coming up to him and talking about football or baseball or whatever. Just now, I drove up to Cal's house, and she told me my car was running rough. Cal and I were supposed to have a study date, but, instead, he's under the hood with Cissy looking at my spark plugs! Finally, Cissy said I needed a complete tune-up, and Cal said maybe we should postpone our date until tonight so that he could do it. So I said fine, and I left."

"That was your first mistake," Jessie said, taking a sip of soda. "Never leave the field to the enemy."

"You're right," Lisa said gloomily. "I did it last week, too. Last Thursday night, Cal and I were watching TV in his den and Cissy dropped over. She stayed the whole evening, monopolizing the conversation. I can't talk about sports, so I just ended up sitting there, looking pretty. Not that I'm not good at that. But I'd like Cal to notice me instead of talking to Cissy! I don't know what to do," Lisa said with a sigh.

"Maybe you should be friends with Cissy, too," Jessie suggested. "Instead of resenting her, get to know her."

"I *do* know her," Lisa said. "And we have absolutely nothing in common."

Slater put down his slice of pizza. "I have a better solution, Lisa."

Jessie rolled her eyes. "Advice from Slater? I'd be careful if I were you, Lisa."

"I'm desperate," Lisa said. "I'll listen to anybody."

"Thanks for the vote of confidence, girls," Slater said, annoyed. "I'll be available for apologies after I tell you my solution."

"Okay, Slater, spill it," Lisa said.

"Find her a boyfriend," Slater said flatly. "She can't horn in on your date if she has one of her own."

"Slater, that's a great idea," Lisa breathed. "I *am* sorry I didn't trust you."

"Actually, it's a perfect solution," Jessie admitted. "I apologize, too, Slater. Occasionally, I *do* see a glimmer of intelligence in that brain."

"But who can I get?" Lisa pondered.

Shrugging, Slater picked up his slice again. "I can't do everything for you, Lisa."

"It would have to be someone athletic," Lisa mused. "And someone who liked to work on cars. Not a brain, but not stupid, either. And cute enough so that she can't resist him." Slowly, a smile spread over Lisa's face.

"Slater!" she exclaimed. "You're perfect!"

"Slater?" Jessie asked in a horrified voice.

"Hey, wait a second," Slater said. "What do you mean, not a brain?"

"You're perfect," Lisa said rapidly. "Cissy will love you. You'd make a really cute couple."

"Forget it, Lisa," Slater said, crossing his arms. "I'm not going out with some tomboy with tree-trunk legs who can bench press more than I can."

"But Cissy is *cute*," Lisa said. "She has a great personality."

"Sure," Slater said. "If you like talking about socket wrenches all night."

"So I exaggerated before," Lisa said. "I know you'd like her. She knows more football stats than most guys know."

"Lisa, let me clue you in on something," Slater said. "When it comes to girls, I'm not looking for experts on sports trivia. There are other, uh, attractions I'm more, uh, attracted to."

"Please, Slater?" Lisa pleaded. "For me?"

Slater shook his head. "Sorry, Lisa. I'd climb the highest mountain and swim the deepest sea for you, but I won't do this."

"But you're not dating anybody," Lisa pointed out. "What else do you have to do?"

"Anything," Slater said. "Clean my room. Floss my teeth. Do my math homework. You name it, I'll do it instead of asking out Ms. Macho."

Slater took a big swallow of soda to make it clear that the conversation was over. Lisa had unknowingly opened a very big can of worms, and it was definitely ruining his appetite. He and Jessie were dating again, but they were keeping it a secret. They were tired of their friends teasing them about breaking up and making up so many times.

Right now, a pair of furious hazel eyes were flashing *No way, pal* at him across the table. Lisa had no chance of success when Slater was facing the wrath of Spano.

Lisa sighed and picked a piece of cheese off the pie and ate it. Her eyes narrowed as she watched Slater avoid her gaze. He was just being stubborn, she decided. All he needed was a little push. She'd find a way to get Slater together with Cissy Garlock—whether he wanted to or not.

The door of the Max banged open, and Zack, Kelly, and Screech ran in. They were laughing as they stood in the doorway, shaking the rain off their clothes.

"It started pouring again," Kelly said as she sat down. "It looked like it would clear up for a while. Zack and I even started to play tennis."

Zack squeezed in next to her. "I'm glad it started again. Kelly was winning. I hate that."

"I hope it stops," Slater said.

"It usually does," Jessie said.

"Are you scared of thunderstorms, too, Slater?" Kelly asked.

"Me?" Slater guffawed. "Dream on. I was just wondering about the football field on Saturday. I don't like to play in the mud. It gets slippery out there. No, Kelly," he said, flexing a muscle, "real men aren't afraid of thunderstorms."

"How about ghosts?" Zack asked.

Slater looked uneasy. "Ghosts?"

"I noticed you were pretty scared in class today," Zack said.

"You must have been looking in a mirror, buddy," Slater said. "Your face looked kind of green."

"Cut it out, you guys," Kelly said. "We were *all* a little scared. I didn't know Mr. Belding was so good at telling ghost stories."

"I knew he was pulling our leg the whole time," Slater boasted. "I wasn't scared at all."

"Yeah, right," Zack said. "That's why you were shaking so bad I thought we were having an earthquake."

"You're the one who had to hold your girlfriend's hand," Slater pointed out, grinning. "Listen, preppy, I get on a football field every weekend and face scarier guys than Eerie Eddie. While you're chasing after a little green ball in your little white shorts, I'm being pummeled by guys named Killer."

"You think football makes you braver than the rest of us?" Zack snorted.

"I don't think it, I know it," Slater said.

"Prove it," Zack said.

"Any day, pal," Slater said.

"How about any *night*?" Zack asked craftily.

Jessie frowned. "What are you cooking up now, Zack?"

"Did someone mention food?" Screech asked, bobbing out from behind his menu. "I'm starving. What *are* they cooking up?"

Zack ignored Screech. He had a scheme to call Slater's bluff, and Slater had played right into his hands. "I bet that you wouldn't be able to stay overnight at Bayside High," he said to Slater. "Not with Eerie Eddie on the loose."

"There *is* no Eerie Eddie, Zack," Kelly said. "Mr. Belding said so."

Zack leaned across the table. "What if he was lying?" he said. "What if Mr. Belding saw how much he'd scared us and realized he'd gone too far? What if he told us it wasn't true so that we wouldn't be scared?"

Kelly looked nervous. "I never thought of that."

"We all know that Mr. Belding has no imagination," Zack said. "How could he make up a story like that on the spot?"

"That's true," Jessie said thoughtfully.

Slater gave a hoot of disbelief. "You guys are listening to Morris? I'm telling you, there's no such person as Eerie Eddie."

"Then prove it," Zack repeated. "Stay overnight at Bayside High tomorrow."

"What kind of a sucker bet is that?" Slater scoffed. "That wouldn't be hard."

"So just do it," Zack said with a shrug.

"Okay, preppy. You're on," Slater declared.

"Wait a second," Lisa said. "How will we *know* if Slater spends the whole night? And what about you, Zack? You're claiming to be just as macho

as Slater. How will *Slater's* spending the whole
night at Bayside make *you* more macho?"

"It will just mean that they're both jerks,"
Jessie said crisply.

Suddenly, Zack wasn't too sure that his dare
had been such a good idea. He had to admit he
wasn't crazy about spending the night in a dark,
empty school. But there was no way he could back
down now.

"I'll stay, too," Zack offered. "We'll try to
track down Eerie Eddie. We'll see who goes off running into the night."

"How will we know if you both do?" Lisa
asked. "If I know you guys, you'll *both* get scared
and lie to us and say you spent the night."

"Let's all do it," Jessie suggested. "Let's
watch Slater and Zack try to catch Eerie Eddie."

"No way!" Kelly said. "I'd be too scared."

"Won't it be fun to see Zack and Slater hiding in their sleeping bags?" Jessie asked teasingly.

Lisa giggled. "I can't wait. Count me in."

Kelly sighed. "I guess there's no way I can
miss this."

"Me, too," Screech said, coming out from
behind the menu again. "But what am I not missing?"

"The Battle of the Macho Stars," Jessie said
with a grin.

"Whoa, wait a second," Screech said. "I
know I'm macho, but I don't want to *battle* anybody."

"Not you, Screech," Lisa said, rolling her dark eyes. "The ghost busters."

"Now that's more like it," Screech said, relieved. "Watching videos is my second favorite activity after petting my lizard. I'll bring the popcorn."

"I can't believe I'm doing this," Kelly said.

"Don't worry, Kelly," Jessie reassured her. "We'll all be together. Nothing's going to happen."

"I wish this didn't sound like the beginning of a horror movie," Kelly grumbled.

▲   ▼   ▲

The rain had cleared by the time the gang left the Max. Jessie drove home behind Zack's Mustang. Zack pulled into his own driveway next door to Jessie's house, and they waved as they locked their car doors and headed to their own front doors.

When Jessie got inside the house, she dumped her books on the kitchen table and went straight out the back door. She ran quickly across the wet grass to the Hendersons' yard next door. She cut across their lawn, wiggled through their back hedge, and came out on Dover Lane. Slater was leaning against his Chevy, waiting for her. She flew into his arms.

"Mmmm," Slater said, his cheek against hers. "I've been waiting for this all day."

"Me, too," Jessie said, snuggling closer.

"It's really torture to have to pretend we're not together anymore," Slater said.

"Well, maybe we should tell people," Jessie said, pulling back. "I mean, we're really solid now. We've been together for two whole weeks and we haven't had one fight."

"It's true," Slater said. "We're much too mature for that now."

"We've really grown," Jessie agreed. "We respect each other's point of view and each other's personhood."

"Right," Slater said, even though he wasn't sure what his personhood was, exactly.

"We have a whole new relationship now," Jessie continued. "We share with each other and we're honest with each other."

"Right," Slater said. Jessie was beginning to sound like a new-age guru, but he knew better than to contradict her.

"Besides, I want to bring you to my con-sciousness-raising group, and I can't if we're still a secret," Jessie continued. "We're having a poetry reading in a couple of weeks, and everybody's invit-ing their boyfriends. I'm going to read some of my poems."

Slater laughed. "Whoa, Jessie, you've got to be kidding. You're kidding, right?"

Jessie stepped out of the circle of his arms. "No, I'm not. What's the problem?"

"A *poetry* reading at a *women's* group?"

Slater asked with an incredulous laugh. "A double whammy! I'd have to go to Wimps Anonymous to get over the experience!"

Slowly, the smile faded from Slater's face as he noticed that Jessie wasn't smiling back. Not a flicker of amusement registered on her face.

"Oops," Slater muttered. So much for two whole weeks without a fight.

"I didn't realize you had such a strong attitude about poetry," Jessie said frostily. "Or should I say such a *stupid* attitude?"

"Hey, I'm just being *honest*," Slater said. "Isn't that part of our new relationship?"

"Yes," Jessie snapped. "But *maturity* is part of it, too, remember? Oh, excuse me. You might have to look up that word in the dictionary. Because you sure don't know what it means!"

"Jessie, calm down," Slater said worriedly. "Poetry just isn't my bag, you know that."

"But it's *my* bag," Jessie said. "What have you got against it?"

"Nothing," Slater said. "It's fine for girls and wimps."

"Fine," Jessie said. "If you don't want to associate with wimps or girls, what am I doing here?"

"Girls have their place," Slater said, moving closer to her and trying to slip his arms around her. "Let me show you where."

Jessie slipped out of his grasp and folded

her arms. "Let me tell you something, Slater. You need to learn the difference between being macho and being stupid. Until you do that, I don't know if our relationship has a future after all!"

Tossing her long curls, Jessie stamped off. Slater sighed and crashed back against his car door.

"So much for honesty," he groaned. "Next time, Slater, do what you *used* to do with girls—lie. It might not be good for your personhood, but it's a whole lot safer that way!"

Chapter 3

▲ ▼ ▲ ▼ ▲

Slater decided to do what he always did after a fight with Jessie—sulk. That night, he made a big bowl of popcorn and settled down in front of the TV. There was no way he'd call and apologize tonight. He knew that he'd be doing it soon enough.

When the phone rang as he was flipping channels, Slater let it ring three times just in case it was Jessie. Then, afraid she'd hang up, he ran to it and snatched it up.

"Hello?" Slater put on a happy voice so that Jessie wouldn't think he was sitting around sulking.

"Hi, it's Lisa," Lisa said. "You sound like you're in a super good mood."

"I was just watching TV. What's up?"

"Slater, I really need you," Lisa said. "My car broke down. I managed to get home, but it died in the driveway. Cal was right. I really do need a tune-up."

"Wasn't he coming over tonight to do it?" Slater asked.

"Right," Lisa said. "He, uh, canceled. Can you come over?"

Slater sighed. "Lisa, I told you not to buy that car. It had *lemon* written all over it."

"I know," Lisa said. "But it was so perfect. It matches my favorite lipstick. Can't you come over and look at the motor? I drained my savings paying for it, and I can't afford to fix it now."

"You didn't need my help when you decided to buy the heap of junk," Slater pointed out.

"But I saw my mistake!" Lisa cried. "Please, Slater?"

Slater sighed. "Okay. I'll look at it."

"Super! Can you come right now?"

"Now? Tonight?"

"There's no time like the present," Lisa chirped. When only silence came through the receiver, she added in a cajoling tone, "I'll give you wardrobe tips."

"No, thank you," Slater said. "I don't want to end up in a pink leisure suit."

"I just baked a tray of brownies...."

"Why didn't you say so?" Slater growled. "I'll be right over."

Slater parked in front of Lisa's house. He saw that the garage door was open and the light was on, so he headed down the driveway instead of going to the front door. The night was hot and sultry, and steam was rising from the wet pavement. The clouds parted for a glimpse of a full and luminous moon. It was a very romantic evening, Slater noted sourly. And he was going to spend it bent over a greasy engine.

The first sight that greeted him when he entered Lisa's garage was a pair of long, bare legs in cutoffs. The legs disappeared into a pair of high-top sneakers that looked like they'd been the favorite toys of a very large dog. Slater stopped dead. And here he'd thought that *Jessie* had the best pair of legs in Palisades.

A girl was bending over Lisa's engine, her head underneath the hood. She came out when she heard his footsteps and looked him up and down. He had a confused impression of a scrubbed, freckled face with one smear of grease across the cheekbone and bright blue eyes. Cropped sandy hair stuck up in various clumps as though the girl had recently run her fingers through it.

"Hi," Slater said.

"Who are you?" the girl said.

"Did anyone ever tell you," Slater said, "that you have really good manners?"

"Nope," the girl said.

"I didn't think so," Slater said.

Just then, Lisa entered the garage, holding a plate of brownies. With her was Cal Everhart.

She beamed at Slater. "I see you two have met."

"No, we haven't," Slater said. He couldn't help feeling annoyed. He had a pretty good idea now who this girl was, and he didn't like it one bit. Lisa had tricked him.

"This is Cissy Garlock," Lisa said. "Cissy, meet my friend A. C. Slater."

Slater nodded at Cissy and said hello to Cal. "I thought you needed my help," he said to Lisa. "It looks like Cissy has it all under control." He gave Lisa a nasty look.

"Want a brownie?" Lisa asked innocently.

"I think we just have to replace those plugs," Cissy said. "They're really gunky. I can do it right now, if you want."

She turned her back on Slater and punched Cal in the arm. "You hoarding those brownies, Everhart?"

Slater wondered why such a great pair of legs were wasted on a girl with not one ounce of charm. "Let's get going," he said. "Lisa, do you have a socket wrench?"

"I'll check my purse," Lisa said with a grin.

"I have one," Cissy said. She stuffed the rest of the brownie in her mouth and crossed back to the car.

It only took Slater and Cissy half an hour to tune up Lisa's car. They started it and the engine purred perfectly.

"You guys are the best," Lisa said. "Come on in and have some lemonade."

"I'd better get going," Slater said.

"Don't be silly, Slater," Lisa said. "I have more brownies. You can't turn down brownies."

Reluctantly, Slater followed the rest of them into the Turtles's basement rec room. Lisa put on a record and sat next to Cal on the big green couch. That left Slater to sit next to Cissy on the love seat. Great.

Cissy chewed on a brownie and regarded him thoughtfully. "Hey, wait a second. You're A. C. Slater, the quarterback."

"Right," Slater said shortly.

"Wow," Cissy said. "You played some game last Saturday. That play in the third quarter, when you faked a pass and then drove right through the offensive line—" Cissy slammed her hand down on the arm of the couch. "Pow! Did you call that play or did the coach?"

"I did," Slater said. He had to admit he was flattered. Jessie never even came to football games. She claimed if she wanted to see a bunch of cavemen, she could go to the Museum of Natural History.

"It reminded me of a Joe Montana move," Cissy continued. "That guy is incredible. He's like a dancer and a bulldozer put together, you know?"

"Exactly," Slater said, pleased. He had never said it out loud because it sounded kind of wimpy, but he'd always thought that being graceful was super important for a quarterback.

Cissy tucked her long legs underneath her and reached for another brownie. She started to talk about last week's Forty-niners game, and Slater settled in for a good discussion of offensive strategy.

He was so interested in the conversation that when Cal stood up to go, he was surprised to find it was already ten-thirty. Slater couldn't believe it. He stood up to go, too, and while Cissy wiped down her socket wrenches, Lisa came up to him.

"Offer to drive her home," she hissed.

"What?" Slater asked. "Where does she live?"

"What difference does it make?" Lisa whispered fiercely. "Drive her home and ask her out."

"You sound like a marine sergeant," Slater whispered back. "And I don't take orders."

"C'mon, Cissy," Cal said. "Your mom is probably peeking out your front curtains right this minute."

"I'm out of here," Cissy agreed.

Lisa poked Slater hard. He ignored her. "Nice meeting you, Cissy," he called. "Catch you later, Cal."

With a twinkle in his eye, he said good night to a disgruntled Lisa. There was no way he'd let her manipulate him into asking Cissy out. Even though he'd enjoyed talking to Cissy, he wasn't interested. Jessie was the only girl for him. And if Jessie ever found out that he'd driven Cissy home, he would be dead meat. No, he wasn't about to blow it with Jessie again. He valued his life too much.

▲   ▼   ▲

The next morning, Slater saw Jessie waiting for him by the front stairs of school. That must mean she was ready to make up, he thought in relief. He quickened his step happily.

As he walked up, he saw Lisa cutting across the lawn toward Jessie. Suddenly, Slater realized that he could be in trouble. He couldn't ask Lisa not to tell Jessie about last night. He just hoped that she wouldn't blab about it. But that was like asking ice cream not to melt.

"Hello, beautiful," he said in an undertone to Jessie as he came up.

She gave a shy smile. "Hi," she said softly. "I'm sorry about yesterday."

"Me, too," Slater said.

"I was miserable all last night," Jessie said.

"Me, too," Slater admitted.

Lisa came up, her eyes sparkling and her hair bouncing. "Isn't it a gorgeous day?" she asked.

Jessie looked up at the gray sky. "Not exactly. It's supposed to rain again."

Lisa shrugged. "We need rain. It's good for the crops."

Jessie looked at her, amused. "What crops? This is Palisades. We grow malls here, not food."

"I'm sure there are crops *somewhere*," Lisa insisted, smiling happily.

"You're certainly in a good mood," Jessie observed. "What happened? Yesterday you were lower than Slater's chemistry grade."

"I think I solved my Cissy Garlock problem," Lisa said. "Thanks to Slater, that is."

Jessie looked at her, puzzled. "Thanks to Slater?"

"He had a date with Cissy last night," Lisa said.

"What?" Jessie blurted.

"Lisa, it wasn't a date," Slater said quickly. "You tricked me into coming over and fixing your car. You knew Cissy would be there. It wasn't a date," he repeated, looking into Jessie's eyes.

"Okay, maybe it wasn't a date," Lisa admitted grudgingly. "But you guys sure did get along. You sat on the couch together for an hour and never stopped talking. When are you going to ask her out?"

"Yes, Slater," Jessie said, turning to him, her hazel eyes flashing. "When are you going to ask Cissy out?"

"I'm not!" Slater exclaimed.

"But why?" Lisa asked. She giggled and nudged Jessie. "He didn't take his eyes off her legs."

"Really," Jessie said in a wooden voice.

"Lisa!" Slater barked.

"What?" Lisa said defiantly. "You couldn't. Cal and I both noticed. Cal didn't like it. He's a little overprotective. He's like a big brother to Cissy. Hey, maybe we should double-date."

"I have to get to homeroom," Jessie said stonily.

"Jessie—" Slater said helplessly. He couldn't defend himself with Lisa standing right there. Then their secret would be out, and Jessie would be angry at him for *that*.

"What?" Jessie asked curtly.

"You've got ten minutes before the bell," he said lamely.

"I want to be early," Jessie said through clenched teeth. "Coming, Lisa?"

"Right behind you, girlfriend. I want to check my makeup."

Slater watched Jessie and Lisa walk away. He sighed. This was not going to be his best day, he could tell. Jessie was mad at him again, and tonight he had to walk through a dark and silent Bayside High pretending he wasn't scared of ghosts. One thing he knew for sure—if he ran into Eerie Eddie, he couldn't run to his girlfriend for protection.

▲   ▼   ▲

After school, the gang waited at the Max for Zack to show up. He had promised to find a way for them to sneak into the school that night.

"I wish he'd get here," Kelly said worriedly. "What if he gets caught? I don't know what he's doing, but I know he shouldn't be doing it."

"He *is* taking a long time," Jessie said.

"How hard could it be to open a window?" Lisa fretted.

"With Morris, you never know," Slater said. "He probably has to *reason* with it first."

"Maybe he got caught and Mr. Belding gave him detention," Screech said.

The girls exchanged hopeful glances. They didn't want Zack to have detention, of course. But if he did, that meant that his mission was unsuccessful. Now that they were close to spending the night at Bayside, it didn't seem like such a fun thing to do after all.

Zack burst through the door of the Max and headed for them. "Mission completed, gang," he said. "The gym window is unlocked. It will be a cinch to open it and climb onto the bleachers. We're in."

"What took you so long?" Kelly asked.

"I had to wait until Coach Sonski left," Zack explained. "Is everything all set?"

Jessie nodded. "I'm supposed to be sleeping over at Kelly's house, and so is Lisa. Kelly is supposed to be sleeping at my house."

"And Slater and Screech are supposed to be at my house. I'm supposed to be at Slater's," Zack said.

"I'm bringing my infrared camera," Screech

said. "I'm going to get a picture of Eerie Eddie and send it to the *Paranormal News.*"

Zack looked at his watch. "Okay. Let's synchronize our watches. We rally under the elm tree near the gym window at exactly nine o'clock. Then we'll boldly go where no student has gone before—to Bayside High at midnight!"

Chapter 4

▲ ▼ ▲ ▼ ▲

At exactly nine o'clock, Zack squinted through the darkness at the gang. "Ready?" he asked in a solemn tone.

"Ready," everyone answered.

Keeping in the shadows, they left the protection of the elm tree and sprinted to the side wall of Bayside High. Hugging the wall, they headed to the last window of the gym. Zack tugged at it and pushed it open.

"I'll go in first," he whispered. "Then I'll help Kelly in."

Zack climbed through the window feetfirst. His feet swung in the air, and he felt for the top of the bleachers. As soon as his toes touched wood, he slowly lowered himself down. Relieved, he stood upright. Then he turned and looked up. "Okay," he whispered.

A moment later, Kelly's legs came through the small window. Holding onto her ankles, then her knees, Zack lowered her to the top bleacher. After Kelly was standing safely, he whispered for Lisa to follow.

One after the other, the gang quickly and silently slithered into the gym. Slater was the last one down, and he tossed down their sleeping bags and a knapsack full of snacks that Zack had brought. They all climbed down the bleachers and dumped their gear on the gym floor.

"This is really spooky," Lisa whispered, looking around.

"It's so quiet," Kelly agreed.

"I think it's kind of fun," Jessie said in a normal voice, and everyone jumped.

"Shhhh," Lisa warned.

"Why?" Jessie asked. "There's nobody here. Unless you're thinking of Eerie Eddie," she added with a grin.

"Jessie!" Kelly exclaimed.

"Come on, you guys, let's go exploring," Jessie urged.

Everyone got out their flashlights and started up the stairs in single file. They barely made any noise in their sneakers, and they didn't speak. When Screech sneezed, they turned to him and told him to be quiet.

"Sorry," he whispered. "I got a tickle in my nose."

"So scratch it and be quiet," Lisa whispered.

At first, the dark, empty halls felt eerie and strange. They wandered through classrooms and peeked into the teachers' lounge. But after a while, they got used to the silence and began to speak in normal voices. By the time they reached the third floor, they were a little more relaxed.

"I've got an idea," Slater said. "Let's play eraser soccer in the hall. We've got to take advantage of this."

"That's a good idea," Zack said. It would help ease the tension, that was for sure.

They split into teams and kicked the eraser down the hall, laughing and joking as they scored goals. The specter of Eerie Eddie didn't appear, and soon everyone was able to forget about him.

Finally, Slater kicked the eraser, and it hit Screech's knee and sailed past Kelly to score a goal. The game was over, and Slater's team had won by one point.

"Look, it's almost midnight," Jessie said.

"I'm getting sleepy," Kelly admitted, stifling a yawn.

"Maybe we should go back to the gym," Jessie suggested. "We have to get out of here tomorrow morning pretty early so no one sees us."

"There's a basketball game at nine, so we should head out way before then, in case the coach comes earlier," Zack said. "Let's brush our teeth and wash up and then go back to the gym."

"Oh, well," Lisa said. "We didn't get to see Eerie Eddie."

"And we didn't get to see Zack turn green," Slater joked.

They went back to the gym for toothbrushes and soap, then washed up in the first-floor bathrooms. In only a few minutes, they had returned to the gym, spread out their sleeping bags, and crawled inside them.

"Anyone know any ghost stories?" Jessie asked with a soft giggle.

"Shhh," Kelly said. "I'm just relieved that nothing happened."

"I'm disappointed," Slater said. "I would have liked to tackle old Eddie and teach him a thing or two."

"You can't tackle a ghost," Jessie said.

"I can tackle anybody," Slater boasted. "Or any *thing.*"

"Will you guys be quiet?" Lisa said sleepily. "It's time for my beauty sleep."

Everybody snuggled into their bags. There was no sound, and the darkness pressed even closer around them. It was strange to be lying on the gym floor under a basketball net, but soon, the velvet darkness and the quiet lulled the gang toward sleep.

Then they heard them: footsteps above their heads. Their eyes flew open, and everyone froze.

"Did you hear that?" Kelly whispered.

"No," Lisa said, but her voice was shaking. "I didn't hear those footsteps at all."

"Well, I heard them," Jessie said, sliding her sleeping bag closer to Kelly's and Lisa's.

"Me, too," Zack said.

"I heard them," Slater said. "Did you hear them, Screech?"

"Screech?" Lisa said.

"Oh, my gosh!" Kelly gasped. "Eddie got Screech!"

Zack jumped up. As soon as Slater saw that, he jumped up, too. He didn't know what he was going to do, but he didn't want anyone to think he was a coward. Besides, he should move away a little bit so that no one could hear his heart pounding. It sounded awfully loud to his own ears. Slater walked a few steps away, across Screech's sleeping bag.

They heard a muffled cry, and Screech's head poked out of the bottom of his sleeping bag.

"Ow!" he said. "Somebody stepped on me!"

"What are you doing down there, Screech?" Zack hissed.

"I heard footsteps," Screech explained. "I didn't think they'd land on my head!"

"Shhh," Jessie said. "Listen."

They all fell silent and strained their ears. Footsteps. *Dragging* footsteps, walking back and forth. Back and forth. Slow, scary, eerie footsteps.

"Oh, my gosh," Lisa moaned. "It's Eddie!"

"Let's get out of here!" Kelly said.

"Wait a second," Zack said. "We came here to ghost-bust, didn't we? We have to find out if it *is* a ghost. It could be the wind."

"Right," Kelly said. "It could be the wind wearing really heavy motorcycle boots."

"It could be a security guard," Zack said.

"That's right," Screech said, his curls bobbing as he nodded his head vehemently. "It could. Except that Bayside doesn't *have* a security guard."

"Well, maybe Mr. Belding hired one and we don't know it," Zack said logically.

"If it *is* a security guard, we'd better get out of here fast," Kelly said.

"And if it's Eerie Eddie, we should get out of here faster," Lisa said.

"There's only one thing to do," Zack said. "Somebody has to investigate. If we all go tramping up there, we'll definitely get into trouble."

"Good idea," Slater said. "Only one person should go."

There was a long silence. Everybody looked at Slater. For the first time, Slater regretted that he had such a big mouth. Why had he boasted about tackling a ghost? Then he saw Jessie's scared eyes, and he knew what he had to do.

He swallowed. "I'll go," he said.

"Don't do anything stupid," Jessie said. "Just see what's going on and come right back. Promise?"

"I promise," Slater said. "I'll be right back."

Famous last words, he told himself grimly as he headed up the stairs to the main floor. Wasn't that what the first victim in *Nightmare Terrors, Part Four* had said before he met the guy with the ax?

Slater crept up the stairs noiselessly. His heart sounded like Benny Cracken's big drum in the Bayside Boomers, the school marching band. His legs felt shaky. He didn't know where his next breath was coming from. But he kept climbing the stairs, one after the other. When he reached the landing, he stopped and listened.

The footsteps continued. Step, drag. Step, drag. The weird thing was that he couldn't figure out where they were coming from. They seemed to be coming from *everywhere.* He was opposite Mr. Belding's office, and he walked a few steps toward it. But the footsteps weren't coming from there. Slater stopped again, listening. Now he was positive they were coming from even higher up.

The last thing Slater wanted to do was climb up higher, but there was no way he could return to the gym without checking out the footsteps. His heart was still booming, but now it was in his throat. He could barely swallow, but he squared his shoulders and started to climb.

He paused at the second floor and listened. Now the sound was coming from up higher. From the third floor. The floor that Eddie haunted.

Slater put his foot on the first step. Then the next. He couldn't believe it, but he was climbing. He just had to get to the bottom of this—even if it meant meeting Eerie Eddie face-to-face!

The footsteps seemed to get louder as he climbed. Then, suddenly, they stopped. Slater paused, straining his ears. Nothing. He kept climbing.

There's no such thing as ghosts, Slater told himself determinedly as he rounded the last turning. *There's no such thing as ghosts. There's no such thing—*

Suddenly, Slater yelled in fright. Sitting on the top step above him was a hockey mask!

▲   ▼   ▲

Back down in the gym, the gang exchanged glances. "Did you hear that?" Kelly said.

"It sounded like a scream," Jessie whispered.

"Or a screech," Lisa said.

Screech poked his head out from underneath his pillow. "You rang?"

"Maybe you'd better go see," Kelly said nervously to Zack.

"Okay," Zack agreed. He stood up and started for the gym door. But before he reached it, it burst open and Slater ran in. He held out the hockey mask. The hollow eyes seemed like black holes.

Kelly gave a little scream, and Lisa shrank

back behind Jessie. Screech put his head underneath the pillow again.

"I found it on the third floor," Slater gasped. "All of a sudden, the footsteps just stopped. Then I turned the corner, and there it was."

"It's Eerie Eddie's!" Jessie said.

"Bayside *is* haunted!" Kelly gasped.

"This is incredible!" Zack said.

"It's incredibly scary," Lisa said, her teeth chattering. "Let's get out of here."

The three girls and Screech all ran up the bleachers to the window they'd left unlatched. But nobody could get organized about who would get through the window first. Jessie tried to give a lift up to Lisa, but Screech was already trying to use Kelly as a step as she bent over to give Jessie a boost.

Zack knew he'd better do something before the four of them toppled down the bleachers. He quickly ran up to them. "Hold on, you guys!" he ordered. "Wait a second!"

"Wait?" Lisa asked wildly. "For what? To get killed?"

"Didn't we come here to ghost-bust?" Zack demanded. "Didn't we say that we'd try to catch Eerie Eddie?"

"Sure," Jessie agreed, her hazel eyes wide. "But we didn't think there *was* an Eerie Eddie."

"The situation has changed completely," Kelly agreed.

"Screech, what about you?" Zack said, turning to him. "You brought your infrared camera and everything."

"I know, Zack," Screech agreed, "but what if Eerie Eddie is green? He's probably covered in really gross slime."

Zack put his hands on his hips. "Are you guys going to wimp out, or are you going to help Slater and me?"

The four looked at each other. "We're going to wimp out," they all said.

"Over my dead body," Zack said.

"Zack, that's just what we want to avoid," Screech pointed out. "That's why we're leaving."

"Come on, you guys," Zack said. "We'll all go together. Nothing will happen. If there *is* a ghost, he's just trying to scare us."

"And he's succeeding," Lisa muttered.

"Just imagine what heroes we'll be on Monday," Zack said in a wheedling voice. "The ghost busters of Bayside High. And Slater already promised to confront Eddie himself. Are we going to let him go alone?"

Slater looked up from the bottom bleacher. "Alone?" he asked. His voice came out kind of scratchy, so he cleared his throat. "I mean, I'll go alone if necessary. I said I'd track down that ghost, and I will."

But Zack noted that Slater didn't look as sure as he tried to sound. He was shifting nervously from one foot to the other. Zack knew the macho man was quaking in his high tops. All *right!*

"We can't let Slater go alone," Jessie said. "Zack's right."

"We're in this together," Kelly said with a sigh.

"I'll never forgive myself for this, but I'll stay," Lisa grumbled.

"I'm glad you're finally seeing it my way, girls," Screech said. "Now stop being such sissies and follow me. I'm not scared at all. Zack's right. Nothing's going to happen. But will somebody please promise to look after my hamsters if anything does?"

Chapter 5

▲ ▼ ▲ ▼ ▲

Zack suggested that they split up into pairs to cover more ground. He and Screech would investigate the third floor, Kelly and Lisa the first floor, and Jessie would accompany Slater to the second floor.

Lisa and Kelly hesitatingly made their way to the first floor. They inched down the hallway, clutching each other.

"Do you see anything?" Lisa whispered.

"No," Kelly whispered.

"Me, neither," Lisa said. "Let's go back to the gym."

"Let's just go to the end of the hall," Kelly suggested nervously. "It would be too embarrassing to quit now."

"Right," Lisa said. "Even though nobody would *know* if we quit."

"I'd know," Kelly said.

"I'd know, too," Lisa said. "But I wouldn't exactly *care*. I'm not out to prove anything. I never said I was brave. As a matter of fact, I'm *not* brave. Not a bit. As a matter of fact, you could say that I was an out-and-out coward. I—"

"Lisa!" Kelly hissed. She dug her fingers into Lisa's arm.

"Oh, no!" Lisa exclaimed, looking down at her arm.

"Did you see it?" Kelly whispered.

"See what?" Lisa asked. "I just noticed that you really need a manicure, girlfriend."

"Lisa, look!" Kelly urged. She pointed a shaking finger at the lockers to the right of them. An icky green slime was oozing out of one of the lockers and dripping down to the floor.

"Oh, no," Lisa moaned. "Tell me I didn't see that."

"What should we do now?" Kelly asked, afraid to move.

"What else, girl?" Lisa said. "Scream!"

▲   ▼   ▲

Up on the second floor, Slater decided that he was glad to have Jessie at his side. That way, he *had* to act like a hero. And somehow, acting brave made him feel brave. Well, almost.

He had to admit, though, that being scared

was doing wonders for Jessie's disposition. She was clutching his hand for dear life and sticking close to his side. She hadn't made a sarcastic comment in the past half hour. This ghost-chasing business wasn't too bad, after all.

They started on the west end of the second floor and peeked into classrooms and closets and bathrooms.

"This is so spooky," Jessie whispered as they closed the door to the physics lab. "Do you really think there's a ghost, Slater?"

"Of course not," Slater said. "There're no such things as ghosts." But he snapped his mouth shut. He remembered what had happened the *last* time he'd said that.

"Actually," Jessie said, nervously following the path of Slater's flashlight, "there's been all these studies conducted about paranormal phenomena. There's a lot that can't be explained out there. Even scientists say so."

"Right," Slater said sarcastically. "Like I'm going to listen to some hippy-dippy, crystal-carrying weirdsomobile with a ghost-o-meter." He snorted. "Come to think of it, it would make a great profession for Screech."

"You know, Slater, whenever you don't understand something, you make fun of it," Jessie said. "Just like with the poetry reading. You won't learn anything new about anyth—" Jessie stopped dead. "Slater," she said in a wobbly voice.

"What?" Slater asked, closing the door to a classroom.

"Isn't over there where Eddie supposedly landed?" Jessie croaked. "When he fell over the third-floor railing and the chemistry books fell on top of him?"

"Yes," Slater said, squinting through the gloom. He waved his flashlight around the stairway, but everything looked perfectly normal. "So?"

Jessie grabbed the flashlight and shined the light on the floor. "So there!"

Jessie's hand was shaking, and the light wobbled over a stack of chemistry books right where Eddie must have fallen. The books were covered in cobwebs—and some dark red stuff that Jessie didn't want to know about.

She screamed and clutched Slater. He put his arm around her and they slowly backed down the hall. They heard footsteps pounding up the stairs. Jessie screamed again.

Zack appeared at the top of the stairs, and Jessie collapsed against Slater in relief.

"Are you guys okay?" Zack asked.

"We're fine," Slater said. "But look." He flashed the light on the stack of textbooks, and Zack bent down to look at them.

"Gross," he said. He turned back to them. "I'm going to tell Screech to get his camera and take a picture of this. Are you two going to be okay?"

Jessie nodded shakily. "We're okay."

"I'd better check on Kelly and Lisa. Screech thought he heard a scream coming from the first floor, too. He's probably still hiding in the bathroom. You guys should probably head back to the gym. We'll all rally there."

"Sounds like a great idea," Jessie said, relieved.

Zack ran back down the stairs, and Jessie and Slater turned and started back down the hall to the west staircase. Jessie kept her hand firmly in Slater's.

"I'm so glad you're with me," she whispered.

"You finally see that you need a man around once in a while," Slater said. "If I spent all my time at poetry readings, how would I build up the muscles to protect you?"

Slater knew he was in trouble when Jessie disengaged her hand from his. "The trouble is," she said tartly, "I happen to want a few brains along with those muscles. Not to mention consideration. Maybe one day you'll figure that out. I can get downstairs fine without you, thank you very much."

Jessie stomped down the stairs. She was even too mad to be scared, Slater realized. He guessed he'd put his foot in his mouth again. At the rate he was going, he'd either have to shrink his foot or stretch out his lips. This was getting painful.

He sighed and stopped at the first floor. Might as well take a detour to see what Kelly and

Lisa had found, he thought, inching into the hallway. Everything seemed quiet. Slater wondered if Kelly and Lisa had checked the administration offices. He doubted it. He didn't want to do it, either. But his reputation was on the line. He had to survive this night as a macho man. Especially since Jessie was claiming that it wasn't important.

Slater decided to poke his head into Mr. Belding's office first. He turned the knob slowly, then pushed the door open.

The office looked like it always did. Mr. Belding's desk was as prissily neat as it usually was. His disgusting old maroon cardigan was hanging on the clothes rack, like it always was. Slater drifted farther into the room. Something was different, though, he thought. He just wasn't sure what it was.

Then he noted that the red light of the PA system was on. That was weird. Slater went over and switched it off, then noticed that the micro-phone had been moved. It was pushed to one corner of the shelf, and the flexible neck was bent over in an odd angle. That was even weirder. Mr. Belding always lined up everything perfectly before he left each evening. Everybody knew that. Slater pushed the microphone back again and noticed that it was positioned over a cassette tape player.

Slater punched the eject button and a tape popped out. It was labeled "FOOTSTEPS."

"So that's it!" Slater breathed. Someone had piped in the sound of footsteps over the PA system on the third floor. That was why it seemed to echo like that! But who could have done it? And why?

Slater peered closely at the label. This time his blood pounded with anger, not fear. It was in Zack's handwriting!

▲   ▼   ▲

Back in the gym, Kelly, Lisa, and Jessie were huddled together in Jessie's sleeping bag.

"I wish the boys would get back," Lisa said.

"Me, too," Kelly said.

"We don't need them," Jessie said. "We can take care of ourselves."

"Right, Jessie," Kelly said. "And you're shaking because you're trying out a new dance craze."

"I wonder where Zack put those snacks," Lisa murmured.

"How can you think of food at a time like this?" Kelly demanded.

"I get hungry when I'm scared," Lisa defended herself.

"Oh, for heaven's sake," Kelly grumbled. She reached over and dragged Zack's knapsack closer. She stuck her hand in it and began to rummage through it.

"Eewww," she said suddenly, drawing her hand out. "There's something gooey on my hand."

"Don't tell me the chocolate melted!" Lisa said.

Jessie trained her flashlight on Kelly's hand. It was covered in goo.

"That looks like pretty disgusting candy," Jessie said. "I think I'll stick with M&Ms. They don't melt in your hand, you know."

Kelly brought her hand up to her face. "It's green slime," she said, surprised. "What's it doing in Zack's knapsack?"

"That's weird," Lisa said. "It was on one of the lockers before. Why would Eddie leave green slime in Zack's pack?"

"Wait a second," Jessie said. "Maybe Eddie isn't the one who put the slime in Zack's knapsack. Maybe *Zack* did."

"Zack's the one who put the green slime on the locker?" Kelly asked.

"And he's the one who fixed up the books on the third floor?" Lisa asked. "And the hockey mask?"

"He must be," Jessie declared. "But when?"

The girls thought for a moment.

"It must have been when we were washing up," Kelly said. "Remember, he was the last one to come back?"

"That's right," Lisa remembered. "But what about the footsteps? He was right here the whole time. How could he have done that?"

"I'll tell you how," Slater said, coming into the gym. He held up the cassette. "He piped this over the PA system. I checked. It was rigged to transmit to the third floor—and the gym."

"That slime!" Kelly said. She looked at her hand. "I mean, that worm!"

"That snake!" Lisa exclaimed.

"How are we going to get back at him?" Jessie asked, her eyes gleaming.

"By beating him at his own game, of course," Slater said. "Kelly, where did you put that hockey mask?"

"It's right here," Kelly said.

"And here's the tube of green slime and the fake blood," Jessie said, upturning Zack's knapsack.

"Good," Slater said grimly. "Get ready to give that scheming, low-down Morris the fright of his life!"

▲　▼　▲

"Hurry up, Screech," Zack complained. "My batteries are failing. I can hardly see."

"I'm right behind you, Zack," Screech said. "Don't worry, I won't desert you in this hour of need. Unless I see a ghost. Then I'm out of here."

Just then, Zack's flashlight went out. "Darn," he muttered. "Just follow me, Screech."

Screech clutched the tail of his shirt, and Zack inched down the last flight of stairs gingerly. He had had too much fun tonight to end up with a broken neck.

"Zack," Screech said, his teeth chattering. "Did you happen to hear something?"

Zack stopped. "Yes," he said reluctantly. He *had* heard something. But he had already run through his bag of tricks. Whatever was down there wasn't his doing.

Suddenly, a light flashed, and Zack saw an awful sight. A huge figure in a hockey mask stood there. Green slime oozed from the hole where his mouth was. His hands were covered in red stuff. He started toward them, dragging one foot behind him.

"Eeeeeeooooooowwwww!" Screech screamed. He let go of Zack's shirt, and Zack lost his balance and fell backward on the next step.

"Zack!" It was Kelly's voice. But Zack couldn't see her with the flashlight shining in his eyes.

"Don't, Kelly!" he shouted. "Don't come out here!"

The ghost lurched toward him. And then it spoke.

"Why not, preppy?" An all-too-familiar voice sounded muffled behind the mask. "Don't want your girlfriend to see you pass out?"

Then, four flashlights flashed on. Slater slipped off the hockey mask, grinning, as Kelly ran to Zack's side.

She perched on the step next to him. "I got scared when you fell backward. I thought you might have hurt yourself," she said.

"You're lucky I didn't!" Zack exclaimed indignantly. "That's the sleaziest, most low-down trick I've ever seen! You could have killed me!"

"Are you *sure* it's the most low-down trick you've ever seen?" Kelly said. "What about green slime on lockers?"

"And a pile of bloody chemistry textbooks?" Slater said.

"And echoing footsteps?" Jessie pointed out.

"Ouch," Zack said. "I guess you got me."

"We sure did," Kelly said. "And you deserved it. Why did you scare us like that, Zack?"

"I thought it would be fun," Zack said weakly. "And I wanted to see Slater drop the macho act and get really scared."

"Well, we saw who was scared, didn't we, preppy?" Slater said with a wide grin.

"Yeah," Zack said. "We both were."

Slater and Zack burst out laughing. "I guess we're even," Zack said. "That was a pretty good trick, you guys."

"I even scared myself," Lisa said.

"That was some scream, Screech," Zack said. "My left eardrum will never be the same." He looked around, but Screech wasn't there.

Lisa giggled. "I think Screech took off."

"We'd better find him," Kelly said worriedly. "We have to tell him it was all a practical joke."

Zack stood up. "You're right."

They started up the stairs, but they only had to get to the first floor to find Screech barricaded behind a pile of chairs he'd dragged from the administration offices. Quickly, the gang explained what had happened.

"Maybe we should get some sleep," Zack said.

"Are you sure that we've seen the last of your tricks?" Kelly asked him suspiciously.

Zack held up his hand. "I promise."

Just as Zack made the promise, a ghostly music traveled up the stairs. Someone was playing the harmonica.

"Nice going, preppy," Slater said. "Where'd you get the harmonica music?"

"I have to say, it *does* sound pretty creepy," Lisa said with a giggle.

"Oh, Zack," Kelly said. "You *promised.*"

"You don't understand, you guys," Zack said. "I *didn't do this one.*"

Everyone looked at Zack and waited for him to say *Gotcha.* But after a moment, they realized that he wasn't going to. He looked pale and scared.

"I swear," Zack whispered.

"So what do you think we should do, Zack?" Kelly asked, her blue eyes wide. "Investigate?"

The harmonica music rose up eerily around them. Hairs rose on the backs of their necks. They all exchanged frightened glances.

"Are you kidding?" Zack said. "Let's get out of here!"

Chapter 6

▲ ▼ ▲ ▼ ▲

In a burst of panic, everyone raced for the closest exit. But when they got to the door, it was chained and bolted. Zack hit it in frustration.

"We have to go through the gym window," he said. "We're not going to be able to get out any other way."

"B-but the music is coming from downstairs," Lisa whispered.

"We have no choice," Slater said. "Come on."

"Just stick together," Zack said.

They ran toward the closest staircase. They didn't care about making noise anymore, and they clattered down the stairs, running as fast as they could.

Light from their flashlights bobbed and weaved as they ran through the dark hallways, past the boiler room, past the pool, past the gym locker room. Only one short corridor to go and they would turn the corner and reach the double doors of the gym.

Suddenly, the harmonica music grew louder. It echoed down the hall, and Zack realized that it was coming from straight ahead of them. They raced around the corner and saw him.

Eerie Eddie rose up and stood before them. The harmonica gleamed in his hand like a weapon. He was dressed all in white, and his face was shadowed. He started toward them.

This time, Screech was too afraid to scream. Everyone tried to back up, but they were too close together, and they all got tangled up and fell down.

Jessie found herself half underneath Lisa— and closest to Eerie Eddie. She desperately tried to push herself to her feet. She could see ghostly legs coming closer and closer...

Suddenly, a very human hand appeared in front of her face. "Can I help you?" a deep, amused voice with a lilting Spanish accent asked.

Jessie looked up and into a pair of twinkling brown eyes. Was Eerie Eddie supposed to be *handsome*? Jessie wondered dizzily.

She found a hand grasping hers and helping her to her feet. The hand was warm and very strong. Jessie blinked. She had no idea who this guy was. But she knew one thing for sure: This was *not* Eerie Eddie.

"Who are you?" she asked.

Before the boy could answer, the lights suddenly blazed on. Mr. Monza came out of his office and did a double take when he saw the gang on the floor.

"What's going on out here?" he demanded. He searched the faces of the group and let out a groan. "Mr. Morris. I should have known."

From the floor, Zack waggled his fingers in a wave. "Hi, Mr. Monza. Nice to see you."

"Not so nice to see *you*, Mr. Morris. And is that Mr. Powers with you? To what do I owe the pleasure?"

"Just thought we'd drop by and say hello," Screech said.

"What are you doing in my school at this time of night?" Mr. Monza thundered.

Zack stood up slowly and dusted his hands on his jeans. "Well, Mr. Monza, that's a very good question. A very good question."

"I know," Mr. Monza said. "Now, why don't you give me a very good answer?"

"Hmm," Zack said. "Well. I'm sure you're aware that there's a prowler breaking into buildings in the neighborhood. My friends and I took it upon ourselves to ensure that Bayside High was safe from such an intrusion. Disregarding our own safety, we raced to the help of dear old Bayside High. There's so many valuable things here at school—computers, televisions, VCRs. And memories, Mr. Monza. Memories that—"

Zack's voice trailed off. Obviously, Mr. Monza was not buying this.

"There's no prowler in the neighborhood, Mr. Morris," he said. "Except you."

"Ah. Yes. Well, let me come clean, Mr. Monza. There's a big basketball game tomorrow, as you're aware, and we heard that Valley High was going to send a team of pranksters over here. So we decided—"

But Zack stopped again. Mr. Monza *definitely* wasn't buying it.

Kelly decided it was time to rescue Zack. Only the truth would do it, and she knew Zack would never resort to that.

"It was a dare," Kelly confessed. "Zack dared Slater that he couldn't last the whole night at school. Mr. Belding told us this ghost story the other day when the power went out. So we all decided to come and do some ghost chasing."

Mr. Monza groaned. "Not that old Eerie Eddie story again."

Jessie nodded.

"Mr. Belding trots that out every once in awhile. He made the whole thing up."

"That's a relief," Lisa said.

"He told us that, but we didn't believe him," Kelly said.

"Now can you explain *your* ghost, Mr. Monza?" Jessie asked. She pointed to the stranger with the harmonica.

"This guy scared us half to death," Zack said.

"Maybe he scared *you* half to death, preppy," Slater growled.

For the first time since they'd known Mr. Monza, he looked uncomfortable. "This is Ramón Calderon. Ramón, meet the troublemakers of Bayside High."

Ramón bowed. "Pleased to meet all of you," he murmured. His eyes swept the group in a friendly way and lingered on Jessie.

"Is he a relative of yours, Mr. Monza?" Lisa asked.

"No," Mr. Monza said. "He is the son of an old friend. Ramón recently arrived in the United States from San Cristóbal."

"That's in Central America, right?" Lisa asked.

"That's right, Lisa," Jessie answered. She turned to Ramón. "You must be relieved that the civil war is finally over."

"I would be more relieved if the right side had won," Ramón answered.

"Listen, kids," Mr. Monza said. "It's my turn for a confession. I'm letting Ramón stay here in the basement until he gets a job and a place to live. And I'd appreciate it if nobody knew, if you get my drift."

"I made it hard for him the other day," Ramón admitted with a grin. "I plugged in a hot plate, and, boom, the power went out."

"It's a good thing Mr. Belding is afraid of the subbasement, where the fuse boxes are," Mr. Monza said. "I think he scared himself with that Eerie Eddie story. If he found out I was harboring an illegal alien, I don't think he'd be too happy. He's a rule-book kind of guy."

"Mr. Monza, our lips are sealed," Zack said.

"So you won't tell anyone about Ramón?" Mr. Monza asked.

"Who's Ramón?" Zack asked with a smile.

"I owe you one," Mr. Monza said to them. "Thank you. He should only be here for a few days. I have friends working on finding him a place to live."

"Is there anything we can do to help?" Jessie asked Ramón.

"No, nothing," Ramón said. "You are very sweet to ask."

Jessie blushed and looked away. Slater scowled. He would like to help Ramón, too, but he didn't like the way the guy was looking at his girl-friend. Not one bit.

As Jessie turned back and smiled at Ramón, Slater suddenly realized that he had overlooked something. There was another huge drawback to his secret relationship with Jessie. How could you lean on a guy for scoping out your girl when she wasn't supposed to be your girl at all?

▲   ▼   ▲

On Sunday, Lisa dug her feet into the warm sand and looked out at the sparkling blue ocean. Behind her sunglasses, her dark eyes were thoughtful.

"What are you thinking about?" Kelly asked her as she rubbed sunscreen on her tanned legs. "You've hardly said a word all day."

"I'm still in a coma after not getting enough sleep Friday night," Lisa said.

"Me, too," Kelly admitted. "How about you, Jessie?"

But Jessie didn't answer. She was lying back on the blanket, her baseball cap covering her face. Kelly lifted it gently and saw that she was asleep.

"I guess Jessie's tired, too," Kelly said with a giggle.

On Friday night, the gang hadn't gotten to sleep until 2:00 A.M. They'd decided to spend the rest of the night in the gym, since they couldn't go home without a lot of explaining to their parents. It had been Zack who pointed out that the explaining they would have to do still wouldn't justify why they'd schemed to stay out all night. They'd probably all get grounded. Parents were funny that way.

Mr. Monza woke them up at six-thirty in the morning so that he could clean the gym in time for the basketball game. The group had ended up waiting for the Max to open at seven, then sat around yawning over their coffee until they could go home.

"How was your date with Cal last night?" Kelly asked, settling back in her beach chair and adjusting her sunglasses.

"Great," Lisa said. "We went to the movies and then went for these huge ice-cream sundaes. It would have been totally perfect if Cissy hadn't shown up to get an ice-cream cone and then walked me home with Cal."

"That girl is definitely turning into a problem," Kelly said.

"You're telling me," Lisa groaned. "What should I do now? Slater isn't interested in her at all. He says he'd rather date Zero, his mechanic."

Kelly smiled. "Cissy doesn't sound like the feminine type."

"She's not," Lisa said. "She's really cute, but she comes on like a Mack truck. She's got a great figure, but you'd never know it because she lives in sweatshirts. She'd rather recite basketball scores than have a conversation."

"Maybe she's shy," Kelly said.

"About as shy as a bulldozer," Lisa grumbled.

Kelly laughed. "Lisa, she's not a bulldozer or a truck, she's a girl. And it really does sound like she's insecure. She probably doesn't know *how* to talk to boys. She's always been a tomboy, so she relates to them on that level. She doesn't realize that when it comes to girls, a seventeen-year-old guy isn't looking for a buddy."

"I guess you're right," Lisa admitted. "I don't have much experience with tomboys. I started planning what brand of mascara to use when I was six years old."

"Maybe Cissy needs a helping hand," Kelly suggested. "She needs someone to show her the ropes, help her out. Someone who could write the book on flirting and fashion. That's the only way she'll get a boyfriend of her own."

"Great idea, Kelly," Lisa said. "But who's going to do that? One of her seven brothers?"

"I was thinking about you," Kelly said.

"Me?" Lisa looked at Kelly over her sunglasses. "I want to spend *less* time with Cissy, not more."

"Maybe if you spent a little more time with her *now*, you'd end up spending less time with her in the long run," Kelly pointed out.

Jessie pushed her baseball cap to one side. "Sounds like Kelly makes sense to me, Lisa."

"Okay," Lisa said. "I'll do it. By the time I get through with her, Cissy Garlock will be the most adorable, most popular girl at Bayside High!"

"Whoa, Lisa. Don't get *too* carried away," Kelly said with a laugh.

"Really," Jessie said, adjusting the baseball

cap back over her face. "If you befriend a cobra, don't be surprised if you end up with fangs in your neck."

▲   ▼   ▲

Lisa called Cissy first thing when she got home and invited her on a trip to the mall after school on Monday. Cissy hesitated a minute, but then shyly agreed.

On Monday afternoon, Lisa immediately steered Cissy to her favorite clothing store.

"They have so many cute things here," Lisa said, flipping through the rack. "Blue is your color. It will bring out your eyes. You have fantastic eyes and the longest eyelashes. You'd really look stunning with mascara."

"I don't like makeup," Cissy said. "It feels like a mask on my face."

"Then you're wearing too much," Lisa said. She tilted her head and studied Cissy's face. "All you'd need is a little brown mascara and a smidgen of lip gloss. It would make all the difference."

"Really?" Cissy said.

"I'll show you what I mean after we go shopping, if you want," Lisa offered. "And I've got a few tricks to show you to help with your hair. Mousse is definitely in order."

"Gosh," Cissy said. "I wouldn't want you to go to any trouble. You're so busy with Cal and everything."

Lisa held a sky blue top against Cissy. She gave her a dazzling smile. "Oh, it's no trouble, hon. No trouble at all."

Chapter 7

▲ ▼ ▲ ▼ ▲

At lunch on Wednesday, Screech ran up to the gang in the cafeteria, juggling a thick stack of envelopes. He skidded to a stop by their table. Leafing through the envelopes, he began to hand them out.

"What's this?" Zack asked. "I didn't know we were pen pals, Screech."

"Nanny is having a pool party on Saturday," Screech explained, handing an envelope to Kelly. "She asked me to help her hand these out."

Nanny Parker was the gossip columnist of the *Bayside Beacon,* the school paper. She and Screech dated pretty steadily, and Screech was crazy about her.

"A pool party!" Kelly exclaimed, opening the round invitation, which was shaped like a swimming pool. "I'm psyched!"

"But it's Wednesday," Lisa protested. "I only have two and a half days to decide between my red tank suit or my new two-piece with the little skirt. That reminds me—is Cal invited?"

Screech nodded. "Sure."

Lisa tapped a polished fingernail on the invitation. "Do you think Nanny would do me a favor and invite a friend of mine?" she asked. "She's a junior."

"I'm sure she would," Screech said. "She's got plenty of food, and her backyard is huge."

"I'm not talking about Namu the Killer Whale," Lisa said. "Just a normal-size teenager."

"You're not thinking what I think you're thinking, are you?" Kelly asked Lisa.

Lisa nodded. "I am thinking it. I think."

"You're going to invite Cissy Garlock?" Kelly asked incredulously.

"But this is your chance to be alone with Cal!" Jessie pointed out.

"Yeah," Lisa admitted. "But on Monday at the mall, I talked Cissy into buying a new swimsuit. Now I just have to talk her into wearing it. It's really sexy."

"Lisa, I'm behind you one hundred percent," Slater said fervently. "I definitely think Cissy should come."

"It's really the only polite thing to do," Zack agreed.

Kelly smacked Zack playfully. "I'm going to bring a blindfold for you," she said.

Jessie looked daggers at Slater. He realized that he'd made a very stupid remark. "Of course, I don't notice things like swimsuits," he said quickly.

"Right, Slater," Lisa said. "Tell me another one. Anyway, once all the guys get a look at the new Cissy, I'm sure she'll have a million offers for dates. Especially after I teach her how to flirt."

"Sounds like a good plan," Kelly said. "It will really boost Cissy's confidence, too."

Jessie turned to Screech. "Screech, do you think Nanny could invite just one more person?"

"What is going on with you girls?" Zack asked, laughing. "Why don't you have your own pool party?"

"I just thought that Ramón might like to go," Jessie said. "He's been cooped up in that basement all week."

"That's a great idea, Jessie," Screech said. "I'm sure Nanny won't mind at all."

Now it was Slater's turn to give Jessie a dirty look. But Jessie only spooned up the last of her yogurt, unconcerned.

The bell rang, and everyone gathered their books. Slater drifted close to Jessie as she swung her backpack over her shoulder.

"What's going on with you and Ramón?" he asked.

One eyebrow went up. "What do you mean?"

"Why did you get Screech to invite him?" Slater asked.

"Because I thought he'd have fun at the party," Jessie answered calmly.

"Come on, Jessie, you know what I mean," Slater said impatiently. "Now you'll spend all your time at the party trying to make Ramón feel comfortable. I won't get to see you at all."

"I didn't think you'd even notice I was there," Jessie said with acid sweetness. "After all, you'll be too busy drooling over Cissy Garlock's new bikini." She waggled her fingers in Slater's face. "*Hasta la vista,* baby."

▲   ▼   ▲

Saturday was bright and sunny, a perfect day for a poolside party. Nanny had spent the morning decorating the tables around the pool with inflatable miniature palm trees and hibiscus flowers. Her mother was going to grill chicken, peppers, and onions, and the guests would roll them up in soft flour tortillas for fajitas. Nanny had made guacamole and tons of salsa.

Screech had arranged to go to the party with Zack and Slater, and he nagged them so much about being late that they ended up being fifteen minutes early. They found Nanny in the kitchen, wearing a pair of pink overalls over her swimsuit. She peered at them worriedly behind her wire-rimmed glasses.

"Do you think we'll have enough food?" she asked Screech as she nervously counted the bowls on the counter.

"You'd have enough if the Third Battalion showed up," Screech said, giving her an adoring smile.

"Then again," Zack added, "you invited Slater, so you might want to order in."

Slater quickly swallowed the chip he'd snitched from a big bowl by his elbow. "I don't know what you mean."

"The next time you play innocent, you might try wiping the guacamole off your shirt," Zack said, handing him a napkin.

The doorbell rang, and Nanny jumped. "The guests are here," she said, her nerves fluttering. "What should I do? Should I put out the chips right away? Or should we start with a game of volleyball?"

"Actually, I think you should start with opening the door," Screech advised masterfully.

Nanny left the kitchen, and Screech turned to his friends. "It's great having a mature relationship," he said.

"Right, Screech," Slater said. "Now grab your turtle water wings and let's head outside."

Soon the doorbell was chiming every few minutes as more kids arrived for the party. Slater waited impatiently for Jessie to arrive. When she did, he saw that she had come with Ramón.

Scowling, Slater turned away. He was trying not to be jealous of the guy, but he had to admit he was ready to lose it. But he couldn't let anyone see it. He had to stay cool.

Jessie mingled in the crowd around the pool, introducing Ramón to the kids. Slater watched her out of the corner of his eye. She was wearing a green tank suit with a chiffon sarong tied around her hips. Her long hair was loose today, and it fell down her back in lush, springy curls. Slater wished she didn't look quite so gorgeous.

Grabbing a handful of chips, Slater headed over to where Lisa, Kelly, and Zack were standing.

"Doesn't Cissy look great?" Lisa asked.

"Fantastic," Slater said, even though he hadn't noticed. He'd been too busy staring at Jessie. But now he looked over and saw that Cissy did look pretty great. She was wearing a blue bikini top with her denim mini, and her hair looked different, slightly curled and tucked behind her ears.

Nanny rushed over to the group, wringing her hands. "Nobody's having fun. I'm going to die if this party isn't good!"

"Everyone just got here, Nanny," Kelly said reassuringly. "Just give them a chance. They'll loosen up."

"Somebody should break the ice," Nanny said.

"I will," Screech volunteered. "Is it in the kitchen?"

"No, I mean, somebody should jump in the pool or something," Nanny said.

"I'll do it," Slater said. "I'm ready for a dip." He slipped his T-shirt over his head and tossed it onto a chair. Taking a running start, he cannonballed into the pool. When he came up for air, he saw that other kids were diving in. "How about a game of water volleyball?" he called.

"I'll play!" Cal said.

"Me, too," Cissy said.

"I don't want to get my hair wet," Lisa said.

Slater and Cal were appointed captains and set up teams. Slater wasn't about to stand around the pool waiting for Jessie to notice him! He was going to have fun today. And he didn't want to notice how Ramón stuck to Jessie's side like glue. Any minute now, he would stop sneaking looks at the two of them.

The water volleyball game was a fierce competition, and Slater was exhausted by the time his team won. He climbed out of the pool and reached for his towel. When he turned around, he saw Cissy behind him.

She grinned. Water drops sparkled on her eyelashes, and her eyes were sky blue and gorgeous.

"That was fun," she said, looping her towel around her neck. "You're a terrific athlete, Slater."

That Lisa, Slater thought. *She must have given Cissy those flirting lessons.* But he couldn't deny that they worked.

Out of the corner of his eye, he saw that Jessie and Ramón were directly behind them. Jessie must have heard Cissy flirting with him. Slater saw her move closer to Ramón.

"Do you want to go for a swim, Ramón?" she asked.

"Yes, I would like to," Ramón said. He took off his shirt, and Nanny, who was standing next to them, gasped.

"Where did you get that scar?" she asked.

Her voice carried, and conversation around them stopped as everyone turned to look at Ramón. He had an ugly, puckered scar that ran down his side and disappeared under the waistband of his cutoffs.

"I got it in San Cristóbal," he said shortly. "Just an injury, nothing major. It's not as bad as it looks. Maybe the doctor could have done a better job sewing me up." His white teeth flashed.

Jessie smiled at him, and jealousy swept over Slater. He couldn't handle one more minute of standing around watching this guy take over his girl.

"I've been sewn up more times than I can count," Slater said to Cissy in a voice loud enough for Jessie to hear.

"You have?" Cissy cooed. She reached over and touched his forearm. "I see one scar right there," she breathed. "How did you get it?"

"Football," he said. "Some guy clipped me, and I landed pretty hard."

"Wow," Cissy said. "You have to be *really* brave to play football, I guess."

"It's the toughest sport there is," Slater agreed. "Your body takes an incredible amount of punishment. And Coach Sonski doesn't let you quit, either. Play through the pain, he always says."

Cissy widened her eyes. "That is incredibly brave," she said.

She was overdoing it a tiny bit, but Slater didn't care. Jessie was listening, and Ramón was looking uncomfortable. He probably didn't know that American guys could be macho, too.

Slater pointed to his knee, where a three-inch scar went down to his calf. "And you shouldn't play in shorts. I got this in a pickup game at the beach."

Cissy giggled and touched that scar, too. "Why are those big guys rushing at you all the time?"

What a bogus question, Slater thought Cissy knew more about football than he did, practically. Was this the same girl who had coolly dissected Forty-niner strategy last week?

"They don't want me to score," Slater said. "And they'll do whatever it takes to stop me. Football is like life—it's all pain and glory. That's how you learn how to be a man. Blood and guts. That's what it's all about." He looked at Ramón. "A man has got to stand up and show courage, not hide away underground."

He saw Jessie's eyes flash in anger. She turned away with a disgusted look on her face. *Okay, maybe he'd gone a little too far. But he was too jealous to think straight.*

He saw her bend closer to Ramón, who had put his shirt back on and was standing stiffly at her side, his dark eyes cloudy. Jessie whispered something to him, and he nodded. Then she spoke quietly to Nanny, and the next thing he knew, Jessie and Ramón had left the party—together.

Yeah, Slater thought. *He'd definitely gone too far this time.*

Chapter 8

▲ ▼ ▲ ▼ ▲

"I should really apologize for Slater," Jessie said to Ramón as she drove her car through the streets of Palisades. "He acted like a real jerk."

"I understand him," Ramón said simply.

Jessie glanced at him quickly, then looked back at the road. "What do you mean?"

"He loves you," Ramón explained. "And he is jealous of me."

"He was still a jerk," Jessie said. Then she sighed. "Look, Slater and I were a couple once. But we used to fight all the time."

"And now?"

"Now, well...we're trying to work it out. But we don't want anyone to know. We just want to be together without any pressure for a while."

"I will keep your secret," Ramón said.

Jessie smiled. "I know you will."

"And now will you tell me where you're taking me?"

"To the beach," Jessie said. "There's a place I think you'll like. You haven't seen enough of Palisades, I bet."

"I haven't seen much," Ramón admitted. "Mostly, I go out at night right now. Mr. Monza is afraid of getting caught by your Mr. Belding."

"Mr. Belding is a good guy," Jessie said, turning onto Ocean Boulevard and heading south. "But I don't know what he'd think about Mr. Monza hiding you."

Jessie drove for twenty minutes until there was a turnoff onto a small asphalt road. She bounced down the road and pulled off into a makeshift dirt parking lot near a clump of trees. There were only a few cars parked, and there was plenty of room for her Toyota. She turned off the ignition.

"Not too many people know about this beach," she explained. "It's not an easy climb down the cliffs. But it's worth it."

She led the way down a twisting path through the trees. After a few minutes, they reached the top of a cliff. Below them, the ocean sparkled in greens and deep blues. The crescent-shaped beach curved between two outcropping hills that gave some shelter from the wind.

"It's called Smuggler's Cove," Jessie said.

Ramón stood, looking around at the hills

and the sea and the sky. The breeze ruffled his dark hair, and his gaze was far away.

"This is amazing," he said in a soft voice. "It looks like my country, where the mountains meet the sea." He turned to Jessie, and she saw that his eyes were wet.

"You miss your country, don't you?" she said.

He nodded. "Very much." He spread out his arms to embrace the beautiful scene in front of them. "This is a gift you've given me," he said. "Thank you."

"It's not over yet," Jessie said, smiling. "Let's climb down."

It seemed natural to hold Ramón's hand occasionally as they navigated the path down the cliff. It was the clasp of friendship, not romance. But still, Jessie couldn't help wondering if Slater would think that, too. Not that she cared right now what he thought. He had deliberately embarrassed Ramón at the party. It just wasn't like him.

They reached the soft sand, and Jessie kicked off her shoes. She reached into her backpack and took out the big beach towel she'd brought to Nanny's party. She spread it out on the sand and motioned to Ramón to join her.

They sat, looking out at the ocean. The beach was practically deserted. A couple lazed in the sun a few hundred yards away, and several solitary people sat sunning or reading a little way down the beach.

"What did you do in San Cristóbal, Ramón?" Jessie asked. "Were you a student?"

"I was in my first year at the university," Ramón said. "I was studying journalism. My father is the editor of a newspaper in the capital of San Cristóbal. My mother is a doctor."

"Did your parents stay in San Cristóbal, then?" Jessie asked.

Ramón nodded. "They thought I should study in the United States. I was sent to my aunt in Los Angeles, but when I arrived, she wasn't at her address. None of the neighbors knew where she went. So I didn't know what to do. I found an organization called Friends of San Cristóbal. I just walked in off the street, and Mr. Monza happened to be volunteering that day. I don't know what I would have done without him. I didn't expect it to be so hard to get settled. The housing is so expensive. And wages for undocumented workers are so low."

"I'm sure things will work out," Jessie said. "You'll be able to go back to school and study."

"I hope so," Ramón said. "Mr. Monza is trying to get me a job washing dishes in a restaurant. I don't know how I can save enough money doing that."

"Maybe you could get a scholarship," Jessie said.

"You can't get a scholarship without papers, Jessie," Ramón said gently.

"There has to be some solution," Jessie said stubbornly. "We have to find someone to help you."

"You have a big heart, Jessie," Ramón said. He turned and looked at her. "I don't blame Slater for being jealous. You are a woman to be treasured."

A deep thrill shot through Jessie. Ramón had a way of speaking that was simple and beautiful. Why couldn't Slater say things like that instead of *Lookin' good, momma?*

"What do you think about poetry, Ramón?" she blurted. "Do you like it?"

"Very much," Ramón said.

"You don't think it's wimpy?"

He frowned. "Wimpy? I don't know that word."

"Soft," Jessie said. "Feminine."

"Ah, it's a good word, then," Ramón said.

"No," Jessie said, laughing. "Not at all. It's what guys call each other when they want to be insulting."

"That seems very foolish," Ramón said with a frown. "Every strong man should have a little softness in him, too."

"That's what I think!" Jessie exclaimed.

"In my country, poets are honored like soldiers," Ramón said. "Words can be as powerful as bullets. That's why I want to be a writer."

He said the words quietly, but there was a strength behind them that Jessie could feel as surely as the sand underneath her fingers. If only Slater would stop boasting and bragging and be more like Ramón! Ramón's quiet determination was much more impressive than Slater's swagger.

He was strong, but he needed help. There just had to be a way to give it. Jessie made a private vow that she would be the one to find it.

▲   ▼   ▲

Jessie thought about the problem all weekend. By Monday, she had come to a decision. She got up early and hurried to school. There, she went straight to the *Bayside Beacon* office. Nanny was already there, working on her column. Perfect.

Jessie sank down in a chair next to Nanny's desk. "Nanny, have you ever thought of writing feature articles, not just your column?"

Nanny looked up. She pushed her glasses up her nose and peered at Jessie. "Yes, I have. All the time. But I haven't been able to come up with a good enough topic. Robbie Gerard keeps shooting down every idea I come up with."

"Well, I have an idea," Jessie said.

"Great," Nanny said. "I hope it's good enough for Robbie."

"Oh, it is," Jessie promised. "I have a feeling Robbie will put this story on the front page!"

▲   ▼   ▲

The article on Ramón came out the next day. Nanny had done an incredible job, telling the story of "Eduardo," who was looking for the American dream. His father was the editor of the most famous newspaper in the capital city of San Cristóbal, and he had been raised in an atmosphere of books and culture. But Eduardo might have to spend his days washing dishes.

Jessie pored over the article excitedly. She was sure that if enough kids were touched by it, they would talk to their parents. Somebody would come forward with a better job or a place to live. The story was just too heartbreaking for people to sit by and do nothing.

She was so excited by the article that she sneaked down to Mr. Monza's office during school hours to find Ramón. She knocked on the door softly three times, then three times again.

Ramón opened the door, and she quickly slipped in. "I have something to show you," she said.

He stood stiffly. "The paper? Mr. Monza has shown me already."

"Isn't it great?" Jessie enthused. "I told Nanny all about you, and she did a fantastic job. I'm sure this will help you, Ramón."

But suddenly, Jessie realized that Ramón's face was like a mask. He turned and placed a T-shirt on top of a few clothes in a small suitcase.

"What are you doing?" Jessie asked.

"I'm leaving, Jessie."

"Where are you going?" Jessie asked, bewildered. "I don't understand."

"I know that you do not," Ramón said. "But I must leave. Good-bye, Jessie."

He closed the suitcase, turned, and walked out of Mr. Monza's office. Jessie was too surprised to move as the door shut firmly behind him.

Jessie felt as though she'd been slapped. She sank down on Mr. Monza's desk chair and stared at the place where Ramón had stood only moments before. Why had he been so stiff? It was like he was angry at her for trying to help!

A few minutes later, the door opened, and Mr. Monza walked in. He looked around the room quickly.

"Where's Ramón?" he asked.

"He left," Jessie said woodenly.

"Oh, no!" Mr. Monza exclaimed. He quickly crossed back to the door and opened it. He looked down the hallway both ways.

"It's too late, Mr. Monza," Jessie said. "He left a few minutes ago."

Mr. Monza closed the door and came back again. "Did he say anything?"

Biting her lip, Jessie shook her head. "Nothing. He seemed really upset. I came down to show him the article—"

"Did you have something to do with that?" Mr. Monza asked, frowning.

Jessie nodded. "I was trying to help."

"Oh, Jessie." Mr. Monza sank down in the armchair. "You don't know what you did."

"No, I don't," Jessie said, her voice rising. "And I wish someone would tell me!"

"You may have put Ramón in very grave danger," Mr. Monza said quietly.

"In danger?" Jessie whispered. "But how?"

Mr. Monza leaned forward, his hands clasped. "You must understand this, Jessie. Ramón comes from a country where treachery is around every corner. His father is a leading dissident there. So is his mother. She heads an organization called Mothers for Children. When the civil war ended, both of Ramón's parents were arrested. The best we can hope for is that they are in prison. They could be dead. Ramón barely escaped with his life. If Ramón is deported back to his country, he will surely be thrown in jail, too."

"I didn't know any of this!" Jessie said. "I never wanted to put Ramón in danger!"

"I know that," Mr. Monza said, patting her shoulder. "It's not your fault. You were just trying to help."

"But, Mr. Monza, I didn't use his name," Jessie said desperately.

"But there are enough details in the story to leave no doubt who Ramón is. And you mention the group in L.A. that I volunteer with. If the INS—that's the Immigration and Naturalization Service of the United States government—decides to investigate, the trail will not be hard to follow."

Jessie's eyes filled with tears. "I feel awful about this," she said.

"Don't feel too bad," Mr. Monza said. "Ramón is being cautious, yes. But he has grown up around death squads, and he's learned to survive by acting quickly. That's why he packed and left immediately. I think I'll be able to find him."

"I hope so," Jessie said, wiping at her cheeks.

"Now don't worry. It's just a high school paper. I don't think the article will attract much attention."

"That's true," Jessie said, relieved. "Why would the U.S. government read a high school paper? And nobody listens to teenagers, anyway."

▲   ▼   ▲

Jessie was definitely not a morning person. The next day, she staggered downstairs and reached for the glass of orange juice her mother always left on the counter. She felt her way to the kitchen table, where her mother was sipping coffee and reading the paper before work. Jessie sat down next to her mother.

"'Morning, sweetie," Mrs. Spano said.

"'Morning," Jessie mumbled.

Mrs. Spano smiled. She was used to Jessie in the mornings, and she knew that after Jessie finished her juice, she'd begin to wake up. She folded the newspaper and drew it closer to her face to continue reading an article.

On the other side of the paper, Jessie sleepily scanned the headlines on page two of the *Palisades Gazette*. There was a protest involving a downtown stoplight. There was a feature article on illegal aliens. She took another sip of juice. Next to the article was a boxed, smaller article. The headline read "EDUARDO'S STORY."

Foreboding stole over Jessie. She leaned closer. She squinted at the byline of the story and saw Nanny Parker's name. And in bold print, she saw a small paragraph explaining that the article was reprinted from the *Bayside Beacon*, a local high school paper.

"Oh, my gosh!" Jessie exclaimed, sitting up and spilling her juice.

"What is it, honey?" her mother asked.

"Nothing," Jessie said. "I just thought of something. I have to get to school early today."

Jessie reached for her napkin and mopped up the spilled juice. She didn't want to have to confess to her mother what she'd done. Her mother had just last week given Jessie a lecture on looking before she leaped. She said that Jessie had to learn to curb her impulsiveness.

"Well, don't skip breakfast," Mrs. Spano said. She returned her attention to the paper.

"Okay," Jessie said. She hurriedly grabbed a

banana and went back upstairs to dress. She scrambled into her jeans and a T-shirt and sneakers and practically ran all the way to school.

She burst into the *Beacon* office and saw that Nanny Parker was there.

"Nanny!" Jessie cried. "Did you see the *Gazette* this morning?"

"See it? Of course!" Nanny beamed at her. "Isn't it great?"

"You knew about it?" Jessie asked.

"Of course," Nanny said. "Do you know Kira Robertson? No? She's a sophomore—anyway, her father is Arthur Robertson, the managing editor of the *Gazette.* She showed him my article, and he was already doing a feature story on illegal aliens so he decided to run my story next to the *Gazette's!* This is the biggest break I ever had!" Nanny threw her arms around Jessie and hugged her. "And I never would have gotten it without you, Jessie," she said fervently. "Thank you so much."

"You're welcome," Jessie said dazedly. "Congratulations, Nanny." She left the *Beacon* office numbly.

Palisades is a small town, she told herself. *It isn't like anybody outside of Palisades will read about it. Nothing is going to happen.*

Jessie went through the day in a daze. She tried not to think about Ramón, but he filled her thoughts. Surely nothing bad could happen to him.

Then, after fifth period, she saw them.

Outside of Mr. Belding's office stood two men in gray suits. One had a briefcase. They were standing talking to Mrs. Gibbs, Mr. Belding's secretary. Jessie slowed her steps and listened. *Maybe they were salesmen,* she thought hopefully.

"I'm sorry," Mrs. Gibbs was saying. "Mr. Belding is a very busy man. He's a principal, you know. You'll have to make an appointment."

"We're officers of the federal government, ma'am," the taller man said. He flipped open a wallet and showed her identification. "INS. You'd better get your principal right away. We have reason to believe that he is busy harboring an illegal alien!"

Chapter 9

▲ ▼ ▲ ▼ ▲

Quickly, Jessie spun on her heels and took off. She ran down the stairs, pushing past students, clutching her books to her chest. She finally reached the lower floor and ran down the hall to Mr. Monza's office.

Mr. Monza was sitting at his desk, glancing over some papers when she burst in. He looked over his reading glasses at her.

"Funny," he said. "I didn't hear the fire alarm."

"Huh?" Jessie said.

"Or is it Eerie Eddie again? You look like you've seen a ghost."

Jessie dumped her books on his desk. "I haven't seen a ghost. But I *have* seen two INS agents outside Mr. Belding's office. And they're accusing him of hiding an illegal alien!"

Mr. Monza took off his glasses and rubbed his eyes. He was silent a moment. Then he stood up. "I'd better go see Mr. Belding," he said.

"What are you going to do?" Jessie asked.

"I'm going to tell Mr. Belding that I hid Ramón," Mr. Monza said.

"Where *is* Ramón?" Jessie asked. "Did you find him?"

Mr. Monza shook his head. "No, and I have to say that I'm very concerned. He hasn't gone to any of the contacts I know. I hope he didn't go back to L.A. I hate to think of him on the streets."

"It's all my fault," Jessie said mournfully.

"No, it isn't, Jessie," Mr. Monza said. "You did the right thing. You just didn't have all the information. I should have told you kids more about why Ramón left San Cristóbal. Now I'd better go upstairs and face the music."

"But do you have to?" Jessie cried. "Mr. Belding could fire you."

Mr. Monza's features softened, and he patted her cheek. It was weird to have gruff Mr. Monza look at her so kindly. "You have a good heart, Jessie," he said. "I hope it doesn't carry you away too far one day."

"You sound like my mother," Jessie grumbled.

Mr. Monza laughed. "Then your mother must be very wise," he said, his gray eyes twinkling.

▲   ▼   ▲

Lisa stopped dead in the hallway when she saw Cissy Garlock. Cissy was wearing an outfit Lisa would kill for. As a matter of fact, it looked like an outfit *she* would wear. A hot pink mini was topped with a matching jacket. Cissy had added a yellow T-shirt and an adorable straw hat with a pink ribbon.

"Wow!" Lisa said, going up and circling around her. "Lookin' good, girlfriend."

"Do you like it?" Cissy asked.

"It's dynamite," Lisa said. "Did you pick it out all by yourself?"

Cissy nodded modestly. "I asked your favorite salesgirl at that store if she had anything special there. She showed me this. She'd put it away for you, but I knew that you wouldn't mind."

"Oh," Lisa said. "Well. Gee, of course not. It looks great on you, Cissy."

"It really works, Lisa! The clothes, the makeup, the new attitude. All the things you taught me. Two guys asked me for a date today!"

"That's fantastic!" Lisa crowed. "So when are you going out? This weekend?"

Cissy shook her head. "I turned them down." She made a face. "They're juniors."

"So?" Lisa asked. "You're a junior."

"I really like older men," Cissy explained.

She looked at Lisa shyly. "Actually, there's someone in particular I really like."

"There is?" Lisa said, drawing closer. "Who is it?"

"Well, I don't really want to say right now," Cissy said reluctantly. "You see, he doesn't know I'm alive. But I like him so much, Lisa!"

"Have you talked to him at all?" Lisa asked.

Cissy nodded. "But I don't think he looks at me like a girl," she said.

"Hon, in that outfit, he's going to have to," Lisa said.

"He's too far above me," Cissy said, downcast. "He'll never notice me. I think he has a crush on somebody else."

Lisa began to get a good idea of who Cissy's secret crush was on. It just had to be Slater. She'd seen Cissy flirting with him at Nanny's pool party. And Cissy probably thought that he still pined for Jessie. After Jessie and Ramón had left, Slater had hardly talked to Cissy at all.

Slater was the perfect choice for Cissy, Lisa thought approvingly. Cissy could win him over. He wasn't dating Jessie anymore, so he had to get over her. And what better way than to fall for somebody else? He'd come around once he saw what an incredible fox Cissy was now. Thanks to Lisa.

She took Cissy's arm and steered her into a private corner of the hall. "Listen to me, Cissy," she said sternly. "Don't ever talk yourself down that way.

You're just as good as anybody else. If somebody isn't looking at you, make him look twice. You're a complete knockout and a real sweet girl. So go for it!"

Cissy's face brightened. "You really think I have a shot?"

Lisa nodded. "Absolutely. Don't let anybody stand in your way."

She watched Cissy walk off with a lighter step. Lisa frowned. She hoped Jessie wouldn't mind her fixing up her ex-boyfriend. But Jessie seemed to have fallen hard for Ramón. Lisa just knew she'd done the right thing for everybody.

▲   ▼   ▲

"Want some pizza, Jessie?" Kelly asked after school that day at the Max.

Jessie shook her head.

"Want some of my fries?" Zack offered.

Jessie stirred her diet cola and frowned.

"Some of my whipped cream?" Screech asked.

Jessie stared off into the distance and sighed.

Zack, Kelly, and Screech exchanged glances. Jessie had been in a funk all afternoon, ever since she'd found out that Mr. Monza had been fired.

"Jess, you've got to snap out of it," Zack

said. "We'll find a way to get Mr. Monza back at Bayside. I feel just as awful about this as you do."

"You can't, Zack," Jessie said, her hazel eyes cloudy. "It's not your fault that the article was printed and Mr. Belding found out. That was totally my doing."

"But you were trying to help Ramón," Kelly said gently.

"Kelly, you can try to make me feel better all you want, but Mr. Monza is the one out of a job," Jessie said bleakly. "And Ramón...who knows where he is."

Slater put down his cheeseburger. Suddenly, he wasn't hungry anymore. His heart felt as though it had been pummeled by the entire offensive line of Valley High. He knew Jessie was truly upset over Mr. Monza. But the Jessie he knew would have been fiery and aggressive, pounding her fist on the tabletop and organizing a demonstration outside Mr. Belding's office. But this Jessie was sad and upset.

Because this Jessie was in love with Ramón.

"C'mon, Jessie," Zack said. "This is a once-in-a-lifetime opportunity here. I'm actually offering to buy you your own order of french fries."

Kelly giggled. "Better take him up on it," she advised. "It only happens once in a century."

But Jessie only crumpled her napkin and smiled faintly. "No, really. I'm not hungry."

Slater wiped his mouth with his napkin and stood up. "I gotta get going," he said. "I'll catch you guys later." He put a handful of crumpled bills on the table and walked out.

Zack and Kelly exchanged glances. What was that all about?

Jessie barely noticed when Slater left. She was too busy wondering if her mother and Mr. Monza were right. Maybe she *was* too impulsive. Maybe she did leap before she looked. And it had sure gotten her into trouble. Poor Ramón was probably sleeping on the streets of the barrio in L.A. because of her. She had befriended him and never probed him about his life in San Cristóbal. She should have sensed his pain and been there for him. She should have been a better friend instead of seeing herself as some sort of Saint Jessie, solving everyone's problems. That day at the beach would have been a perfect opportunity to really get to know Ramón.

Jessie sat up, nearly spilling her soda. "That's it!" she exclaimed.

"What's it?" Zack asked. "You want the french fries after all?"

"I know where Ramón is!" Jessie cried. "Catch you guys later!"

In another moment, Jessie was gone, her hair flying as she dashed out of the Max.

▲   ▼   ▲

Less than a half hour later, she pulled into the dirt parking lot at Smuggler's Cove. The sun was gliding lower in the sky as she hurried through the trees to the end of the cliff. The sun was low enough so that she had to shield her eyes as she scanned the beach below. It was deserted.

Disappointed, Jessie began to turn away when she noticed a dark spot far down the beach, in the shadows underneath the cliff. It could be a piece of driftwood, or somebody could have left a blanket. Or it could be a beach bum waiting for the sunset. But it could be Ramón.

Jessie nimbly climbed down the cliff. She struck out across the sand, heading for what she could now see was a person. Within a few yards, she knew it was Ramón. But he didn't turn, or wave, or acknowledge her in any way. Still, she walked on.

She drew up to him. He was sitting on a blanket, staring out at the water.

"So you found me," he said.

"I was worried," Jessie said softly. "Have you been sleeping here at night?"

"The nights are mild," Ramón said "And I can see the stars."

"Ramón, Mr. Monza explained about your parents and what could happen to you if you're deported," Jessie said, twisting her hands. "I didn't know. And I'm so sorry. Everything is my fault. I know you must be really angry at me."

He turned, and Jessie saw that there was no anger in his face. "But I'm not angry at you," he said. "I'm grateful to you. You cared, and you tried to help. I'm sorry I didn't say that the other day.

I was afraid. I thought I would never be afraid again like I was in San Cristóbal. But that day, it all came back. Maybe it will never go away."

Jessie sank down into the sand next to him. "I hope it will," she said.

"So do I," Ramón said. "Jessie, I appreciate everything you tried to do for me. But it's time I moved on. I'm going to try Los Angeles again."

"But where will you stay?" Jessie said. "What will you do?"

Ramón shrugged. "I'll find something."

Jessie leaned toward him. "Ramón, I got you into this, and I'm going to get you out," she declared.

He smiled at her. "Jessie, you are very sweet. But there's nothing you can do."

"But there is something I could do," Jessie said. "Something foolproof. Something that could keep you in this country for good."

Ramón frowned. "What?"

Jessie took a deep breath. "I could marry you," she said.

Chapter 10

▲ ▼ ▲ ▼ ▲

Ramón stared at her for a long moment. Then he shook his head. "No," he said quietly. "You cannot do that."

"But I can," Jessie said. "I just turned eighteen. It's perfectly legal."

"I don't care if it's legal, Jessie. It's wrong," Ramón said.

"If it saves your life, it can't be wrong," Jessie argued. "Ramón, I couldn't stand it if you got deported."

"I won't get deported," Ramón said. "I'll disappear into Los Angeles. They'll never find me."

"But what will happen to you?" Jessie demanded. "You won't have a place to live or a job."

"I will find a way," Ramón said stubbornly.

Jessie put her hand on top of his. "Ramón, listen to me," she said urgently. "I *want* to do this. It's the only solution. Please let me help you."

"What about your boyfriend?" Ramón asked, searching her eyes. "What about Slater?"

Jessie drew back. "He'll understand."

Ramón laughed softly. "Maybe you should ask him first."

"I don't need to ask his permission," Jessie said, lifting her chin defiantly.

Ramón smiled. "No, you don't need his permission," he said. "But perhaps you might need his blessing."

▲   ▼   ▲

When Lisa got home that afternoon, she saw the light blinking on her answering machine. She pressed play and heard Cal's voice. Sighing, she leaned against the wall to listen.

"Lisa? Hi, it's Cal. Listen—about our date tonight...I'm going to have to cancel. I'm real sorry. It's family stuff, and you know how that is. I'll see you at school tomorrow, okay?"

Lisa sighed in disappointment. She'd been looking forward to their study date all day. And it wasn't studying she was looking forward to!

The phone rang, and she snatched it up. "Cal?"

"It's Cissy. Hi, Lisa."

"Oh, hi, Cissy," Lisa said. "What's doing?"

"Listen, I just had to call and thank you for

our talk today. You are a true-blue friend. You gave me so much encouragement."

"Oh, Cissy, don't mention it," Lisa said warmly. "You know I'm glad to help. Besides, you don't need me to encourage you. You've got good stuff there, girl. Just use it."

Cissy giggled. "I have. And I think it might be working."

"Ooh, do tell," Lisa said, settling down into her red armchair for some gossip.

"Mmmm, I'm not ready to talk about it yet," Cissy said. "I just wanted to tell you that things are definitely looking up."

"Fantabulous!" Lisa said. "Good luck."

"Thanks, pal," Cissy said.

Lisa hung up, smiling. Kelly's idea to make Cissy over had been a brainstorm. And the best part of the plan was that she'd actually made a friend.

Lisa rose and went back to the hall table for her purse. As long as she wasn't seeing Cal, she might as well run a couple of errands before settling in with her studies. She'd noticed a definite gap in her nail polish selection this morning.

Lisa was hesitating between two colors at the Sav-U-Cash Drugstore when she saw Jessie heading down the aisle, her arms filled with shampoo, conditioner, and deodorant.

"Jessie! Hi! Do you like blushing peony or Catalina sunset?"

"Gee, I don't know," Jessie said doubtfully. "They're both pretty."

"You're right," Lisa declared. "I'll get both."

"I was just heading for the register," Jessie said. "My mom asked me to pick up a few things for her. She's working on a big case, and she doesn't have time to breathe." Jessie's mother was a super-driven district attorney.

"Have you been able to find Ramón?" Lisa asked as they walked down the aisle together.

Jessie dropped her shampoo and picked it up again. "Um, yes," she mumbled.

"And he's okay?"

"He's fine," Jessie said. "I talked him into going to Mr. Monza's house. Mr. Monza didn't think his wife would want Ramón to stay with them since they have six kids, but she was glad to take him in."

"That's good," Lisa said. "I sure wish we could do something to help him, though."

"Mmmm," Jessie said. She didn't want to tell Lisa about her decision. Ramón was right. She needed to talk to Slater first. Even though things had been kind of weird between them lately, she owed it to him.

It was time to change the subject. "So how are things going with Cissy?" Jessie asked as she handed over her items to the clerk.

"Oh, I'm glad you asked," Lisa said, putting her nail polish on the counter. "I almost forgot. I wanted to ask you something. Cissy has a major crush on Slater, and I wanted to know if it bothered you. I mean, I know you guys have broken up, but I just want to make sure you're not still carrying a torch. I really think Slater is interested. He was flirting with Cissy like mad at the party."

"I noticed," Jessie said tightly as she pocketed her change.

Lisa pushed her items down the counter. "So would it bother you if Cissy went after Slater? They'd make such a cute couple. And I just talked to her before I came here and she said she was *definitely* making progress. She must have seen Slater after school."

A deep flush stole over Jessie's face, and she turned away to hide it. "She told you that?"

"She sounded very excited," Lisa said, handing her money to the clerk. "So do you mind?" she asked again.

Jessie picked up her bag. "Of course not," she said, forcing a smile. "Slater and I are ancient history. Why would I mind?"

▲　▼　▲

She didn't owe Slater an explanation after all, Jessie thought furiously as she drove home that night. Not one word. He was flirting with Cissy Garlock behind her back. Obviously, he considered the relationship over. He was already lining up his next girlfriend.

When he didn't call her at all that night, she

knew she was right. He was probably on the phone with Cissy!

But if she didn't owe anything to Slater, Jessie knew she owed it to her friends to tell them what she was planning. The next morning before school, she walked next door to Zack's.

He was just getting into his Mustang, and he stopped when he saw her walking across the lawn.

"Can I hitch a ride?" Jessie called.

"Sure," Zack said. "Did your car break down?"

"No," Jessie said. "I just wanted to talk to you. Are you picking up Kelly?"

Zack nodded. "Hop in."

Jessie climbed into the front seat, and Zack backed out of the driveway. "So what's up?" he asked as he steered toward Kelly's house.

"Um, let's wait until we pick up Kelly," Jessie said. All of a sudden, she was awfully nervous about telling Zack and Kelly her news. Yesterday, with the sun setting on the beach and the troubled look in Ramón's dark eyes, it had seemed like the right thing to do. It had seemed romantic and brave. But today, underneath the bright sun, heading for another ordinary school day, it didn't feel as right. As a matter of fact, it felt a little foolish.

Kelly waved from her porch and ran toward

the car. "Hi, Jessie!" she said as Jessie got out to slide into the backseat. "You're going to ride with us today? This will be fun. Did you have car trouble?"

"She wants to talk to us," Zack said.

"Oooh, that sounds serious," Kelly teased.

Jessie smiled weakly, but she didn't say anything. Kelly was probably expecting Jessie to discuss something at school or a new crush. She didn't know that what Jessie had to discuss *was* pretty serious.

"So what's up?" Kelly prodded.

Jessie leaned forward, her arms on the front seat. "I found Ramón yesterday," she started.

"Is he okay?" Kelly asked, concerned.

"He's fine," Jessie said. "But he doesn't know where to turn next. Those agents are on his trail, and Mr. Monza can't keep him at his house forever. So I came up with an idea."

Zack coasted to a stop at a red light. "That's good news," he said.

"What's your idea?" Kelly asked, her blue eyes bright and interested.

"I'm going to marry him," Jessie blurted.

For a long, horrible second, there was silence in the car. The light turned green, but Zack didn't move. A car honked behind them.

"That's the stupidest idea I've ever heard!" Zack roared.

"It is not!" Jessie yelled. "Maybe if you'd listen to me, you wouldn't fly off the handle!"

The driver of the car behind them honked more insistently, but Zack didn't even hear him. He twisted around and stared at Jessie. "If you're not kidding, you're crazy!"

"I'm not kidding, and I'm not crazy!" Jessie said. "And if you'd just listen for one—"

"Why should I listen to a crazy person?"

"Zack!" Always the peacemaker, Kelly gently put her hand on Zack's arm. "Don't yell at Jessie," she said. "And pull over before the driver behind us beats you up."

Zack stepped on the gas and slowly steered the car over to the side of the road. He twisted around again and gave Jessie an incredulous look.

"Don't look at me like that," Jessie said.

"I can't help it," Zack said. "I can't believe what I'm hearing."

"Jessie, there has to be another way," Kelly put in gently.

"Well, there isn't," Jessie said stubbornly. "I got Ramón into this mess, and I have to get him out."

"What about Slater?" Zack asked.

Jessie's jaw set. "Slater? What does he have to do with it?" she asked.

Kelly and Zack exchanged glances. "Jessie, he still cares for you," Kelly said. "It's obvious. I don't know if you're blind, or he's blind, but you guys need to talk."

"Kelly, you're wrong," Jessie said. "Slater is interested in Cissy Garlock."

"Cissy?" Kelly frowned. "I didn't hear anything about that."

"Talk to Lisa," Jessie said grimly. "She'll tell you all about it. Look, you guys, this is my decision, and I've made it. I'm getting married."

"What about your mother?" Zack asked desperately. "Have you told her about this?"

"Not yet," Jessie said, tossing her head. "But I'm not worried. My mother has been going on marches for San Cristóbal for two whole years. She writes letters to the government there trying to get political prisoners released. I'm sure she'll support me one hundred percent."

"But—" Kelly started.

"Jessie—" Zack started.

"That's enough, you guys," Jessie said flatly. "I've made my decision. Nothing you can say will change my mind. Anyway, we'd better get to school."

Zack put the car in gear and pulled out into traffic again. Nobody said another word.

What could he say, anyway? Zack wondered in despair. Jessie was determined. And he knew his friend well. When she believed that something was right, she didn't let anything get in her way.

But this wasn't about introducing recycling at Bayside or protesting offshore drilling on Palisades Beach. This was Jessie's life. And she was making a wrong decision, Zack was sure of it. Somehow, he had to find a way to stop her.

▲   ▼   ▲

Later that day, Zack cornered Slater by his locker and told him what Jessie was planning. Slater's mouth hung open for a full ten seconds. Then he snapped it shut and shrugged.

"It's her decision," he said.

"What are you talking about, man?" Zack said. "It's a terrible decision. The worst."

Slater turned back to his locker and took out his chemistry book. "But it's Jessie's decision," he said. "You know Spano as well as I do, Zack. She's going to do what she's going to do, no matter what we think. We can talk to her until we're blue in the face, and all we'll get is...is a bunch of blue faces. And Jessie will be Mrs. Ramón Calderon."

"I'm not talking *we*," Zack said. "I'm talking *you*."

"Me?" Slater said gruffly. "What do I have to do with it?"

"Slater, don't try to con a con man," Zack said. "Kelly and I both know you're still crazy about Jessie. Something's going on between you two. I don't know what it is, and it's your business, but you can't let her do this."

"Zack, I repeat: There's nothing going on with me and Jessie, and even if I *was* still crazy about her, there's nothing I could do to stop her from doing something she wanted to do."

"So you won't even try?" Zack asked in despair.

Slater slammed his locker shut. "No. I won't even try."

Zack paused. "Then you're stupid, man," he said finally. "Maybe it's time you got off that macho act and acted like a human being. Maybe it's time you admitted that you care."

Slater stood there, hitting his book with the palm of his hand. He had never been so furious with Zack in his life. He had been irritated at him—and momentarily annoyed. But he had never felt so close to punching his friend in the face.

"I've got to get to class," he said finally.

Zack didn't move. "Slater—"

"Get out of my way, Zack," Slater said evenly. He shouldered past him and walked away.

Chapter 11

▲ ▼ ▲ ▼ ▲

After school that day, Lisa was heading for cheerleading practice when she heard her name called. She turned and saw Cissy running toward her. She looked adorable in faded jeans, a little pink T-shirt, and suspenders with tiny hearts on them.

"Great outfit," Lisa said approvingly. "I'm glad we picked out those suspenders."

"Me, too," Cissy said. "Listen, Lisa, I know I'm probably bugging you all the time. But I really need some advice. Do you have a minute?"

"Sure," Lisa said. "Shoot."

"I wanted to know...well—" Cissy blushed and looked down.

"What, Cissy?" Lisa asked. "Don't be shy. It's only me. Things are looking up, you said."

"Well..." Cissy looked up again. The expression in her sky blue eyes was uncertain. "They were. But now they're moving as slow as a Dodge Dart with a bad tranny."

"Huh?" Lisa asked.

"Dead stop," Cissy explained. "I'm going to see him this afternoon, and I wanted to know..."

"Wanted to know...," Lisa prodded.

"I wanted to know how you get a guy to kiss you," Cissy blurted. Then she blushed.

Lisa bit her lip so that she wouldn't laugh. She didn't want Cissy's fragile new self-esteem to crumble. "Okay," she said seriously. "Let me see. Hmmm. First of all, you've got to look into his eyes. Don't keep looking away from him. Just stare into his eyes like this." Tilting her head, Lisa put on a dreamy expression.

"Okay," Cissy said, nodding. "I can do that."

"Then, let's see...You have to touch him while you talk to him. Casually, like this." Lisa put her hand on Cissy's arm briefly.

"But what should I talk about?" Cissy fretted.

Lisa shrugged. "Oh, it doesn't matter. A math test. Your parents bugging you. Your dog— who cares? Better yet, let *him* do the talking. Just make sure you keep eye contact and physical contact."

"Eye contact, physical contact. Right," Cissy said. "What else?"

"Okay, here's another thing," Lisa said.

"When he *looks* like he wants to kiss you, stand your ground. You'll be really nervous, but *don't move*. Don't change the subject, don't laugh, don't fidget, don't *do anything*. Stand there and keep looking at him! And part your lips, like this." Lisa tilted her head again, put on the dreamy expression, and parted her lips just a fraction.

"Now you do it," she said.

Cissy tilted her head, put on a dreamy expression, and parted her lips.

"Perfect!" Lisa said. "There's just one more thing. Actually, it's probably the most important thing."

"Okay," Cissy said, giving a serious nod. "I'm listening."

"If all else fails," Lisa said with a grin, "kiss him first!"

▲   ▼   ▲

Slater grunted as he threw himself at the dummy in football practice. He hit it with such force that the dummy flipped over and Slater landed on top of it.

Coach Sonski blew his whistle and walked over to Slater. He stood over him, hands on his hips. "Are you having a problem I should know about, Slater?"

Slater got up and dusted off his knee pads.

Picking up the dummy, he righted it and gave it a pat. "Just hitting hard, Coach, the way you tell us to."

"I didn't tell you to smash my athletic equipment," the coach said sourly. "Are you having a personal problem? You're going overboard today. You ran ten extra laps without me ordering you to."

"I have a lot of energy today," Slater said, running in place.

"And you knocked out Greg Tolan's contacts."

"I apologized," Slater said. "I didn't mean to hit him so hard. Really, Coach, nothing's wrong."

Coach Sonski put his hands on his hips. "You tried to tackle a Toyota, Slater!"

"It was green with a gold interior," Slater said sheepishly. "Those are the Valley High colors."

"It was my car!" the coach roared.

"Sorry, Coach," Slater mumbled.

Coach Sonski sighed. "That's enough for today, Slater. Hit the showers. And make it a cold one!" he yelled after him.

Back in the locker room, Slater slipped out of his shoulder pads and kicked off his cleats. Ever since Zack had told him about Jessie, he hadn't been able to see straight. He had tried to work it out in football practice, but he hadn't been able to get Zack's words out of his mind.

Maybe it's time you got off that macho act and acted like a human being.

Slater slammed his hand against his locker. What was the matter with everybody, anyway? Zack was sounding just like Jessie. The world was going totally crazy.

He showered and changed into shorts and a T-shirt. Maybe a run on the beach was what he needed to clear those words out of his head. It was Slater's favorite cure when he was upset.

As he left the locker room, he saw Lisa at the water fountain, taking a break from cheerleading practice.

"Hey, Lisa," he said as he headed for the door.

"Hi, Slater," she said offhandedly, turning to take another drink. Then she suddenly turned back. "Slater! What are you doing here?"

"Why shouldn't I be here?" Slater asked. "I had football practice."

"But what about Cissy? Aren't you seeing her this afternoon?"

Puzzled, Slater shook his head. "Why would I be seeing Cissy? I haven't seen her since the pool party."

"You haven't? I mean, you aren't—I mean, you don't—"

"I haven't, I aren't, and I don't," Slater said. "Does that clear it up for you?" He waved a good-bye and headed for the exit.

Lisa stared after him. "But if you don't," she said, frowning, "then who do?"

▲   ▼   ▲

Slater decided to skip Palisades Beach, where he was sure to see people he knew. He didn't want to have to talk to anyone. He just wanted to run. He headed down the coast to Smuggler's Cove. The small beach was usually deserted, especially during the week.

Slater climbed down the cliff, noting that there were only a few people on the beach. Good. He walked down to the hard sand by the edge of the water and began to run. The salty breeze felt good against his skin. Maybe it would blow his troubles out of his mind. He ran hard, his legs pumping, and began to work up a sweat. After the run, he'd go for a short swim. Who needed Jessie?

Suddenly, Slater broke his stride. A guy in cutoffs was coming out of the water just ahead of him, pushing his wet, dark hair off his forehead. He locked eyes with Slater. It was Ramón.

Anger coursed through Slater as he trotted closer. Ramón started to say hello, but Slater cut him off. "I heard what you're planning with Jessie," he said. "I think it stinks."

Ramón didn't say anything. He stood there, watchful and expectant. He must have sensed that Slater was ready to explode.

"And I'm warning you not to do it," Slater said, taking a step closer to him. He was bigger than

Ramón—and stronger. He would make toast out of the guy. "If you don't leave Jessie alone, you'll have to answer to me."

To Slater's surprise, Ramón didn't move an inch. He didn't back up, and he didn't seem nervous, either. He stood on the sand, his bare feet planted far apart, and held Slater's gaze.

"I know that you care about Jessie," he said. "And I can understand why. But you cannot make decisions for her."

Slater knew that. Jessie had pounded it into his head often enough. But he wasn't about to let some squirt tell him so!

"It's none of your business what I do," he said menacingly. "Just listen to what I'm saying. Back off. *Comprende, amigo?*"

"Perhaps you would have more success with Jessie if you spoke to her instead of me," Ramón said. "And if you spoke out of love rather than anger. But that's your business. I'm not afraid of you, Slater. I've known worse bullies than you. Much worse."

"Oh, here comes that macho act again," Slater said. "I saw you at the pool party, acting all mysterious about your scar. You don't fool me for one second, Ramón. I know a phony when I see one. You probably got that scar falling off your pony. You just wanted Jessie to feel sorry for you."

"No," Ramón said. "I don't want anyone's pity. And I didn't mean to be mysterious. I didn't think the story should be told at a party. It's not that kind of story."

"What kind of story is it?" Slater taunted. "Did you get an appendicitis attack while you were studying poetry at school?"

Ramón looked away, over the water. "We heard only moments before they arrived that they were coming," he said quietly. "A friend, a colleague of my father's, warned us. We had only moments before we heard the squad pull up in front of our house. We knew they were coming to arrest all of us, maybe to kill us on the spot. My mother hid me underneath a pile of blankets. She told me that no matter what, I must not look out. I must remain quiet. She could not bear, she said, to be in prison knowing I was in prison, too. It would help both of them if they knew I was free. Plans had already been set in motion to send me to the United States, plans I had resisted. But I promised her that day, as I heard the sound of their boots running up the walk, that I would go. That I would not look out, no matter what I heard."

Ramón kept his eyes on the horizon. It was like he was speaking to himself. "I heard them come in. I heard their boots. I heard their orders. I heard them breaking things, all my mother's beautiful crystal. I heard them destroying the house. And then I heard the sound of blows—and a cry. Just one. They were asking for me, and my parents were saying I was at the university or with friends, they didn't know where. I heard them searching the house. Then I heard the sound of shooting. I heard the bullets around me. They were shooting in the closets, under the bed, trying to get my mother to betray where I was. They shot into the pile of blankets."

Slater jumped. His gaze was fastened on Ramón's face.

"The bullets hit my side and my arm. I didn't cry out. I bit right through my lip. Then I heard more shooting and the sound of something being dragged. It was my father or my mother—or both. And still I did not look. I had promised my mother I would give her a reason to live. I would give her life—or her death—meaning. I would survive."

Ramón turned his gaze back to Slater. "That was the hardest part, worse than the bullets. I heard my parents being dragged out of the house, and I don't know if they were dead or alive."

Slater didn't know what to say. He had never been faced with so much suffering. He had never even glimpsed such courage. Now, looking at Ramón, he saw what Jessie saw. And for the first time in his life, he realized what real machismo was all about.

Chapter 12

▲ ▼ ▲ ▼ ▲

On Friday morning, Jessie left for school at her usual time. But instead of heading for Bayside High, she drove to downtown Palisades and parked outside the city hall. She had already arranged to meet Ramón here. They had to find out exactly what they needed in order to get a marriage license.

Jessie thought they might require blood tests. She'd have to look for a doctor in the yellow pages. If everything went right, they could be married here that very weekend. Or she could think up a story for her mother, and she and Ramón could cross the border into Nevada. She'd find a way.

She got out of her car nervously and headed up the steps. Her mother's office was in one of the city government buildings, and Jessie prayed that she wouldn't run into her. Despite what she'd told

Zack and Kelly, she wasn't sure that her mother would back her up at all.

Jessie crossed her arms and waited by a pillar for Ramón. She told herself not to be nervous. This was the only thing to do.

She felt a hand on her shoulder, and she jumped. "Ramón!" she said, turning around.

But it wasn't Ramón. It was Slater. "What are you doing here?" she asked nervously. "Why aren't you in school?"

"Look who's talking," Slater said.

Jessie's lips pressed together. "Don't try to talk me out of this, Slater. I've already made my decision."

He nodded. "Okay. But don't you think you owed it to me to tell me your decision yourself? I thought we were a couple. Remember what you said about honesty and sharing?"

"Wouldn't you rather be *sharing* with Cissy Garlock?" Jessie snapped.

Slater frowned. "That's the second time I've heard that. Why does everyone think I'm interested in Cissy Garlock?"

"You mean you're not?" Jessie asked, surprised.

"Not at all," Slater said.

"What about the pool party?" Jessie asked suspiciously. "You were flirting with her like mad."

"You were there with Ramón. I was trying to make you jealous."

"You were jealous?" Jessie asked.

"Well, yeah, of course," Slater said. "You're my girl, Jessie. When I see you with someone else, it drives me crazy. That's why you can't marry Ramón. I'd go completely over the edge. You'd have to check me into a loony bin."

Jessie sighed. "Oh, Slater. I was so mad at you that day. When you said you wouldn't go to my poetry reading, it was like you were rejecting *me*. My poetry *is* me, Slater. It comes from the deepest part of me. And when you say you're not interested in that, it really hurts. You're always talking about my looks. It made me feel like that's the only thing you were interested in."

"Jessie, why didn't you tell me that?" Slater asked.

Jessie's eyes were full of unshed tears. "I guess I just wanted you to know it without me telling you." One tear trembled on her eyelashes and slipped down her cheek.

"That's not fair," Slater said, feeling helpless. "You know what a blockhead I am," he said. But Jessie didn't smile.

The old Slater would have gotten angry. He would have said that it wasn't his fault, that Jessie should have told him how she felt. But Ramón was right. He had to learn how to talk to Jessie out of love, not anger. And Zack was right, too. Slater had to get off his macho act and show Jessie he really cared. No wonder Slater had been so furious at Zack. The guy was right on.

Slater grabbed Jessie's arms. "I love you,

Jessie Spano," he said fiercely. "And it's not because you're beautiful. I love your hair and your legs and your smile, but they could all disappear tomorrow and I'd go right on loving you. I love what's inside you. I love the fire and the softness and the strength. I love your heart. And I love your soul."

"Oh, Slater," Jessie said. "That's so beautiful!"

She threw herself in his arms, and he held her close. Then he kissed her, a nice, long kiss.

Jessie drew away. She wiped her cheeks and smiled at him. "I hate to say it, but we still have a problem. I promised Ramón that I'd marry him. I can't back out."

"Ramón backed out himself, Jess," Slater said.

"What?" Jessie asked. "How do you know?"

"Because he told me. We had a long talk, actually."

"A talk?" Jessie asked suspiciously. "Did you threaten him?"

Slater grinned. Jessie knew him all too well. "Well, at first I did," he admitted. "But then we really talked. I learned more about his life in San Cristóbal. And you're right, Jessie. He can't go back there. We have to find a way to keep him in the United States legally."

"We?" Jessie asked.

"We," Slater repeated determinedly. "I want Ramón to stay in the United States, too. But I don't want to lose you in the bargain. Ramón sent me here to tell you that he can't marry you. But I have another idea. Look, Jessie, if you have a problem with the law, who do you go to for help?"

"A lawyer," Jessie said, shrugging.

"Right. And how about a lawyer who knows all about the problems of San Cristóbal and will be sympathetic? Someone who goes on marches and writes letters and really cares? Oh, and somebody who just happens to have a loony daughter?"

Jessie laughed. "My mother. I should have asked her to help long ago."

He held out his hand, and she took it. "I already made an appointment," he said. "Ramón is waiting for us there. Let's go."

▲   ▼   ▲

On Monday morning, Zack knocked on Mr. Belding's door. "Come in," he heard Mr. Belding call.

Zack stuck his head in the door. "Good morning, Mr. Belding."

"Uh-oh," Mr. Belding said with a sigh. "I was hoping that this week would start out peacefully. That was my first mistake. What's wrong, Zack?"

"Wrong?" Zack asked. "Nothing's wrong."

"What scheme have you cooked up this week?"

"Scheme?" Zack asked with a puzzled air.

"No scheme. I just came to invite you to Mr. Loomis's history class today. I'm reading my term paper."

"Wait a second, Zack," Mr. Belding said. "Let me get this straight. You're inviting me to class so I can hear you read your term paper?"

"That's right, Mr. Belding," Zack said.

"No catch?"

Zack shook his head.

"No ulterior motive?"

"I thought you might enjoy it," Zack said with a modest shrug. "And I thought that it would be a good idea for us students to include you in our academic pursuits."

Mr. Belding looked pleased. "Well, well. That's very nice. Very nice. I'll be there, Zack. Thank you."

"Thank *you*, Mr. Belding," Zack said.

Mr. Belding showed up at Mr. Loomis's class promptly after lunch. Zack was already in the front of the room, ready to read. He waved at Mr. Belding as he took a seat in the back of the room.

In a firm, clear voice, Zack read a summary of the current problems in San Cristóbal. Then he outlined the difficulties immigrants from that country faced, comparing them to the difficulties immigrants faced in the early part of the century.

Zack reached the end of the paper and looked up. "I'd like to conclude my paper with a story," he said. "It's the story of a guy who's not very different from me or you. He likes baseball and he's not very good at math. He worked on his high school paper. He's not real good at keeping his room neat, and he likes to go to the beach on weekends. The difference between that guy and us is that he happened to have lived through a revolution, and the bad guys won. His name is Ramón Calderon."

Zack told the story of the day the army had appeared at the Calderons' door. He had already asked Ramón's permission. Zack told the story just the way Ramón had told it. He didn't exaggerate. He didn't have to. The story was powerful on its own.

By the time he finished, he could see that the class was spellbound. Even Mr. Loomis looked moved. There was a minute of stunned silence, and then everyone began to clap. Mr. Belding clapped loudest of all. There were tears in his eyes.

"That was the most terrible story I ever heard," he said. "Anyone who helps Ramón Calderon should be considered a hero."

"Even if that person breaks a rule?" Zack asked.

"Especially then," Mr. Belding said, dabbing at his eyes with a handkerchief.

Zack walked to the back of the classroom and handed Mr. Belding a slip of paper.

"What's this?" Mr. Belding asked.

"It's Mr. Monza's home phone number," Zack said. "I thought you might want to tell him he's a hero who still has a job."

Understanding dawned on Mr. Belding's face. He tucked the paper into his pocket. "I'll tell him," he promised.

▲   ▼   ▲

Everyone celebrated Zack's A on his history paper at the Max after school.

"I should frame this," Zack said, staring at his paper. "I might never see one again."

"I'm so proud of you," Kelly told him. "That was a fantastic idea, to get Mr. Belding to come to class. Now Mr. Monza has his job back."

"Looks like Morris has pulled a few good moves lately," Slater said. He grinned at Zack. He'd already apologized to his friend for being angry at him. It hadn't been easy to tell Zack that he'd been right about everything. But it had been the decent thing to do.

"So what's the latest news on Ramón?" Zack asked Jessie. "Have you talked to him?"

"Last night," Jessie said. "He called right after he got to Miami. He said that his aunt was so happy to see him she cried all the way home from the airport. She didn't know he was alive. She had gotten news that Ramón had been put in prison with his parents."

Using her contacts, Jessie's mother had

tracked Ramón's aunt down that weekend. Pilar Calderon had moved to Miami and had found work as a technician in a medical laboratory. She had been overjoyed to hear that Ramón was alive and had immediately offered to take him in. With her as his sponsor, Ramón was now able to stay in the country legally.

"He's going to apply to school in Miami," Jessie explained, snuggling close to Slater. "He sounded really happy. He said hello to all of you."

"Tell him *ihola!* for us, too," Screech said as the waitress put a plate of french fries down in front of him.

"So what's up tonight, gang?" Zack asked. "Anybody interested in renting a video and coming to my house?"

"We can't," Slater said, with a meaningful glance at Jessie. "We have very important plans."

"What are you guys up to?" Lisa asked.

"We're going to a poetry reading," Slater said.

Zack guffawed. "*You?*" he said to Slater. "Macho man?"

"Hey, poetry isn't for sissies," Slater said. "I'm even thinking of writing some poems myself. I already wrote one."

"You did?" Jessie asked, surprised. "Let's hear it."

Slater put a hand over his heart

"Roses are red,
Club soda fizzes.
I'm sure glad my girlfriend
Isn't a missus."

The gang burst out laughing. "Don't quit your day job," Jessie said, giggling.

Kelly looked around the group, beaming. "See, guys? It just goes to show you that what I'm always telling you is true. Things really *do* work out for the best."

"Dream on, girlfriend," Lisa grumbled.

"Can somebody pass the catsup?" Screech asked. "My fries are getting cold."

"What's the matter, Lisa?" Slater asked. "Are things a little rocky with Cal?"

"I've got enough rocks to fill a quarry," Lisa said. "Listen, I'm really happy that you guys are back together," she said, turning to Slater and Jessie. "Don't get me wrong. But, for my sake, I can't help wishing that things had worked out with Slater and Cissy."

"Why?" Kelly asked.

"Lisa, can you pass the catsup?" Screech asked again, staring sadly at his fries.

"Because then I wouldn't have had to give her lessons on how to be a girl," Lisa explained. "I taught her everything she ever needed to know about mousse. I taught her to shorten her skirts three inches, and I got her to throw away those disgusting basketball sneakers. And I even told her to go ahead and kiss the guy she liked if he didn't make the first move!"

"That sounds like good advice," Zack said. "What's the problem?"

"Naked fries," Screech said. "Big problem. Can I have the catsup, please?"

"The problem is, it worked!" Lisa exclaimed. "Cissy has a new boyfriend."

"So?" Kelly asked. "Isn't that what you wanted?"

"You don't understand, Kelly," Lisa wailed. "Cissy's *new* boyfriend is my *old* boyfriend—Cal Everhart! She got the man of her dreams. Except he's the man of *my* dreams! My teaching worked perfectly."

"Good work, Lisa," Screech said approvingly. "You have the satisfaction of a job well done. You should be proud of yourself. We're all proud of you. Uh, Lisa? I wanted the catsup for my fries, not my shirt. You of all people should know that catsup doesn't go with polka dots...Lisa?"